# VOLUME #1

# The Bad Babysitter

KERRIGAN VALENTINE

Cover by The Spookmaster

Cover images courtesy depositphotos,
Haywiremedia (front), and Mondi.h (back)

ISBN: 1518744907
ISBN-13: 978-1518744907

# CONTENTS

# CHAPTER ONE

"I don't like this place," Brad said grumpily out the window.

Andrew ignored him. There was nothing more his little brother liked to do than complain. Sitting between them in the back seat, Shaggles panted and filled the car with his dog breath. It was not minty fresh.

"Oh, it's darling!" Mom said, lifting her sun visor to get a better view of the city. "Look at those beautiful old houses. What's not to like?"

"It's June," Brad said. "JUNE. Why are there so many pumpkins?"

1

As Dad slowed for a stop sign, Andrew looked at the houses. One had three pumpkins on the porch. "It doesn't look like so many to me," Andrew said.

"They're everywhere," Brad insisted, pushing his dragon cards off his lap rather than put them away in the box. "Some are even carved up like today is Halloween. It's stupid."

"It gives the city some character," Mom said.

Andrew looked again at the house with three pumpkins. They weren't carved. There was also a wire reindeer in the grass, Christmas lights twined around the rain gutter, and a giant plastic Easter egg leaning on the fence.

Brad leaned over to point out Andrew's window. "See? There are more of them right there!"

Pushing his hand away, Andrew said, "So what if there are a few pumpkins? Whoever lives there has everything. See the lights and reindeer? The egg? They just never clean up."

"Smart thinking," Dad said, glancing at the house. "They're always ready for the next holiday."

Brad fell back in his seat and crossed his arms. "It's spooky. This whole place is spooky. That's why it's called Chills Hills."

"It's not spooky," Andrew argued. "I looked it up. It was the last name of the man who founded this city. William Edmund Chills was a soldier. He fought in the Civil War." Andrew had made a list of the battles in which William Chills had fought. He liked making lists.

"Spooky," Brad repeated, just to have the last word.

"Well, I think we're going to be very happy here," Dad said firmly, turning onto another street. "Even Shaggles."

Shaggles would be happy anywhere, just so long as there was a toilet full of tasty water for him to drink. Andrew gave the big brown dog a pat and looked out the window. There weren't pumpkins *everywhere*, but now that Brad had pointed them out, Andrew did notice an awful lot of them. Round pumpkins. Thin pumpkins. Tiny pumpkins. Enormous pumpkins. They were sitting on porches and steps, windowsills and walkways. Some were indeed carved like Halloween was just around the corner.

That was weird. Summer had barely begun.

But Andrew wasn't going to dislike a city purely because of out-of-season pumpkins. In their old house, he had had to share a room with Brad. In the new one, they could each have their own. And his new school had a summer science program that started in just a few days. Andrew loved science. He couldn't wait to go.

"And we're . . . home! Welcome to our new life, Calistoga family!" Dad exclaimed, steering the car up a driveway and stopping outside the garage. Andrew got out fast to see it. The house was blue and had two stories. It was much bigger than their old place, where they were always bumping into each other just to get around.

Shaggles ran around the lawn to sniff everything as Andrew leaned back into the car for his backpack. The moving men had been following in the truck, but they had gotten separated in traffic a long time ago.

Once inside the empty living room, Brad shoved past Andrew to get to the staircase. "First dibs on rooms! First dibs!" Brad shouted.

"Hey!" Andrew ran up the stairs after him.

The backpack weighed Andrew down, and Brad made it to the hallway first. He sprinted into the first room with an open door and yelled, "This is my room! Mine, all mine!"

Huffing and puffing, Andrew peered in. Brad was jumping up and down on the carpet. The little window overlooked the backyard.

Sticking out his tongue at Andrew, Brad sang, "Mine, mine, all mine! Mine, mine, all mine!"

Annoyed, Andrew walked down the hallway to the next open door. Then his annoyance went away.

This bedroom was larger. It didn't have one tiny window but big ones on two walls. The side window had a view of a leafy tree, and the front window overlooked the street. Anyone coming or going on the sidewalk or road would be plainly visible to him up high.

He dropped his backpack to the carpet and turned in a circle to see the whole room. This wasn't good. This was *great*. He had his own private space to read and do experiments. The floor wouldn't be covered in Brad's toys and trash and dirty clothes. It was gross how Andrew's younger brother would pick up muddy socks and put them on instead of getting clean ones from his dresser.

Best of all, there wouldn't be any of Brad's boogars on the walls. This was the most fantastic day of Andrew's life.

Opening his backpack, he dumped out the books. He was just stacking them in the corner when Brad ran in. His jaw dropped. Then he shouted, "I want this room!"

"Sorry, it's mine," Andrew said. "Mine, mine, all mine."

"Give it!"

"No!"

Brad balled up his fists and raised them. Gritting his teeth, he said, "I'll fight you for it!"

"You watch too many cartoons," Andrew said, taking a deep breath to stay calm. He had made a promise to himself to stop hitting Brad when the whining and arguing pushed him over the edge. Hitting him felt good in the moment, but it only made things worse. Andrew got in trouble while Brad still whined and argued. The best thing to do was avoid him as much as possible.

Brad threw a warm-up punch into the air to

show how tough he was. Andrew took another deep breath. He was so sick and tired of Brad the Brat. "I'm not going to fight you. I'm older. I'm bigger. I'll win. Now get out of my room!"

Dropping his fists, Brad tilted his head back and screamed at the top of his lungs. Dad came racing up. "What's wrong?"

"I want this room and Andrew took it!" Brad whined.

"He took the other room first," Andrew said in exasperation. "So I took this one. Then he saw it and decided he wanted this room instead."

"But I want it I want it I want it!" Brad screeched, stamping his foot like he was two years old.

"Stop!" Dad bellowed. He had a short fuse for whining. "If you picked the other room first, then you can't just change your mind and take Andrew's. That isn't fair to him. All you can do is ask Andrew nicely if he would like to switch."

"I want to switch with you!" Brad said, and not in a nice way.

"I don't," Andrew said. "I really like this room."

"Then you have your answer," Dad said to Brad. "Come on downstairs. The truck should be here any minute and we'll dig out your bed and toys." He took Brad away.

This beautiful room belonged to Andrew. He was relieved. Hearing a rumble, he went to the front window. The moving truck had just arrived.

The house across the street also had two stories. In addition, it had a turret like a castle. That was neat. Andrew couldn't see too much else of that neighbor's house because of all the tall trees growing in front of it. There were more trees, bushes, and flowers in that yard than in any other yard visible from Andrew's windows.

The two trees closest to the sidewalk in the

neighbor's yard were shaggy. Thin branches full of leaves fell all the way to the grass. The wind swept the leaves aside and revealed a pair of jack-o'-lanterns around the trunks.

They had been given happy faces. The smiles were so wide that they curled up almost all the way to the eyes. It made the pumpkins look like they had just heard the funniest joke ever told. But the eyes were slanted down and mean.

Something about them made Andrew feel uncomfortable. It *was* a little spooky how people in Chills Hills were ready for a holiday that wouldn't happen for another four months. Where did they even buy the pumpkins? Those didn't usually come into stores until the fall.

Up in the turret room, a curtain rippled even though the windows were shut.

"Andrew!" Mom called. "Come help!"

Forgetting about the pumpkins, Andrew turned away to go downstairs.

# CHAPTER TWO

"IT'S perfect," Mom said on the phone several days later.

It was Sunday afternoon, and blazing hot. Dad had gone to the grocery store to stick his head in the freezers. In the front yard, Brad was throwing a ball in the air and trying to hit it with the bat as it dropped. He still hadn't forgiven Andrew for taking the best bedroom. There were fresh boogars on Andrew's door every morning in revenge.

Andrew was on the sofa in the living room, a cold glass of lemonade at his side as he read one of his science magazines. There was a long article about lion prides. Tomorrow he started his summer school class at Corona Elementary School and he wanted to be prepared.

Maybe he would make friends at his new school. There had been a lot of bullies at his old one. Predator and prey, he thought as he turned a page. The popular kids were the predators, and they preyed on everyone else. Andrew had been prey.

Other kids had had it a lot worse than Andrew did. The predators made fun of them for being too fat or too skinny, or for not running fast in P.E. Andrew was neither fat nor skinny, and he wasn't as fast as lightning but pretty fast all the same. They went after him for being smart, calling him nerd and geek and giggling whenever he raised his hand to answer a question. All through fifth grade, they did badly on their spelling tests on purpose, and flashed their zeroes at each other like it was something to be proud of. It was cool to be stupid in that class.

But Andrew wasn't stupid. He wasn't going to pretend that he was just to make some mean friends. He hoped this school would be different.

"Yes, Brad will be in a program, too," Mom said. She was on the phone with Gramma. "Reading 'n Racing. So he'll get the reading support he needs plus lots of running around time, too. He's going to love it."

Andrew wanted to tell Mom that she was fooling herself if she really thought that. Brad wasn't going to love being in summer school. He was a slow reader, so slow that he had been put in the yellow group last year. That made him mad. He wanted to be in green, the fastest group, but he couldn't keep up. He also wouldn't practice to make himself any faster.

"The school is only three blocks away," Mom said, fanning herself with a calendar as

Andrew tried to concentrate on the article. "She goes over there to pick up her afternoon kids and brings them to her house. It's right on our same street. The program ends at noon and I'll be home at two, so I can walk over there and pick them up."

What? Who was *she*? Andrew stopped reading about lions to stare at his mother.

"Bad dog!" Brad shouted outside. "Shaggles, you give that ball back to me!"

"Someone's on the other line?" Mom said. "Oh, no, just call me back. Bye."

Andrew pounced on her. "*Who* is supposed to pick us up after school?"

Mom fanned herself again. "The babysitter. Mrs. Dritch is very nice. She lives in the big house straight across the street and she's been taking care of children for many years. She'll pick you up with a few other kids and you boys can stay there until I get home."

"Mom, I don't need a babysitter!" Andrew cried. "I'm too old!"

"I don't want you two home alone for that long."

"I'm in sixth grade," Andrew said. Or he would be when school started up for real in September. "I can take care of myself at home for two hours. Make Brad go, but I shouldn't have to!"

"I don't know if it's safe," Mom said.

"I'll call you the second I get home so you know I'm here. I won't open the door if anyone knocks. I won't use the stove. I'll send you a text every fifteen minutes with a picture of what I'm doing! Mom, please!"

"And just what are you going to do for those two hours?"

"I'm going to make myself a sandwich and do my homework. It'll be nice to have a quiet place to get it done. I can't study at a babysitter's house with a bunch of little kids yelling all around me."

Mom looked like she was considering it. He stared at her beseechingly.

"You will call or text me the second you get home," Mom said.

"I will."

"You will not open the door if anyone knocks, unless it is a police officer or a fire fighter. You will not invite friends over."

"I won't."

"You will not touch the stove. Or light any candles."

"I won't."

"You will send a text or call me if there's any kind of problem. If I don't answer, you will call Dad. If there's a real crisis, you will call 911."

"Of course."

"If you break any one of these rules, you will need to go to the babysitter's house with Brad."

"I won't break them, Mom. This is going to be my study time."

"Then we'll try it out, at least for tomorrow." She smiled at him. "You've been very mature lately, Andrew."

The front door opened and banged shut. Brad trudged into the room. He was dragging his bat behind him. "I need someone to pitch," he whined.

Andrew didn't want to pitch. But he needed to keep Mom happy so she wouldn't send him to the babysitter's. "I'll do it."

They went outside. Shaggles had flopped over under the tree to rest. There were two girls across the street at the babysitter's house. They were sitting on the steps of the porch, backpacks over their shoulders. A white van covered in pink, blue, and green smiley faces was parked in the driveway.

Andrew threw an easy, underhanded pitch. Brad swung wildly and missed. "You did it too fast!"

"Throw it back and I'll try again."

Brad kicked it over the grass. The ball stopped several feet short of Andrew, who picked it up and backed away. He threw it, slow and easy, but Brad missed. He glared at Andrew like it was his fault.

"You need to use your batting tee," Andrew said.

"I don't want to use it!"

"Then you aren't going to get any better. Go and get it out of the garage."

"You get it."

"Why should I get it? You're the one who needs it."

"I don't need it! *You* don't need it!" Losing his temper, Brad lifted the bat over his head and threw it into the road. Then he ran for the backyard.

"You have to get that!" Andrew shouted. But Brad didn't come back.

The bat had gone all the way across the street and come to rest in the gutter. Checking both ways for traffic, Andrew walked over to get it. This was exactly why he didn't like to play with his brother. If Brad didn't get something right on the first or second try, he had a fit.

The girls were still sitting on the porch. They didn't talk to each other, or have books to read or anything. All they did was stare at Andrew. "Hi," Andrew said.

"Hello," they said together.

He picked up the bat.

"It's a very nice day, isn't it?" one girl asked.

"Uhhh . . . yeah," Andrew replied. That was a weird thing to say. Grownups talked like that, not kids. "Do you live here?"

"No. Our dad is picking us up soon," the second girl said.

They sat so still, like two dolls side by side. The older one looked about ten years old, and the younger eight or nine. Andrew swung the bat over his shoulder.

"It was nice to meet you," the girls called as he crossed the street to home.

Weird. Andrew was glad that he wouldn't have to go to the babysitter and hang out with those oddball girls. He was as excited about his two hours alone in the house as he was his science class. If he finished up his homework early, he could have the TV all to himself.

As Andrew got back to his yard, Dad pulled up in the car. The trunk was full of grocery bags. Getting out, he said, "Look what I have in the back seat!"

Andrew looked through the window. "You bought a pumpkin?"

"Why not?" Dad got it out and handed it to Andrew. "It'll help us fit in. Stick it up there on the porch railing."

Andrew put it in the corner. It *did* make them fit in, but still . . . Why didn't everybody just wait for October? He liked Halloween as much as anybody else, but what was the rush?

A car drove up to the curb and a man called to the girls on the porch steps of the babysitter's house.

They didn't shout. They didn't run.

Standing up at the same second and in the

same way, they walked calmly and quietly to the car. "Hello, Daddy," they said as they climbed into the back seat.

Up on the porch, the screen door opened. A slim, white hand extended out to wave.

# CHAPTER THREE

**THE** first day of summer school was going better than Andrew could have ever dreamed.

He hadn't been too sure about Corona Elementary at first. There were jack-o'-lanterns in the entryway, and people walking by them like that was perfectly normal. But then he walked into Room 4.

It blew him away. The classroom looked like the laboratory of a mad scientist. Fish swam through green water in a dozen aquariums along the walls. Plants hung from the ceiling, spilling flowers and green tendrils over the sides. There were animal skeletons on stands, and jars full of strange things on the shelves. Instead of desks, there were black tables for the students to sit at with drawers full of beakers underneath.

Then there was the teacher. His name was Professor Beek. He had a big puff of white hair on his head, and another on his chin. On his long table in the front of the classroom was a giant bowl with a thick metal grate on top. Inside was a glowing mass of grayish-green ooze that slid around the bowl and even hung from the bottom of the grate. When a girl asked what it was, Professor Beek explained that the ooze was what happened when a person mixed chemicals carelessly.

Andrew had never seen such a thing in all his life. His hand shot up into the air. "What does it eat?"

"I throw it a cell phone now and then," Professor Beek said, giving everyone a hard stare. "It ate nine of them last year, three belonging to the very same student. I don't like to be interrupted when I'm speaking. If you've got a cell phone on you, shut it off *now*." Phones were jerked out of backpacks and pockets all over the classroom, and turned off hastily.

They would be working on mineral identification in the first week. If everyone did well on Friday's quiz, Professor Beek promised to blow something up. Passing out worksheets and shoeboxes full of minerals and supplies, he told them to divide into groups of three.

Andrew looked around uncertainly. Everyone seemed to know each other already. Clusters of three bent their heads down as he turned in his chair to see the people behind him.

There was a blond boy sitting alone at a back table. He had spread out all of his belongings and put up his feet on the second chair so no one could sit beside him. He did not look friendly.

At the other back table, a boy and girl were pushing their shoeboxes together. The boy saw Andrew and smiled. He had clear braces on his teeth.

He looked much friendlier than the first boy. Getting up with his shoebox, Andrew dragged his chair behind him. "Hey, is it okay if I join you two-"

He tripped over a backpack, which the blond boy had left in the aisle. The shoebox dropped to the floor and the lid popped off. Half of the contents fell out. Embarrassed, Andrew got down to pick everything up.

Rudely, the blond boy said, "Don't kick my stuff, Bigfoot!"

The boy with braces leaned down to help Andrew and said, "Don't leave your stuff in the aisle and people won't kick it."

"This is America, genius. It's the land of the free," the blond boy retorted. "That means I can put my stuff wherever I want."

He opened his shoebox and got to work.

"Oh, don't mind Wally Wonderful," said the boy with braces to Andrew. "Hi, I'm Max, and this is Casey." The girl gave Andrew a brisk nod and wrote her name on her worksheet. She had a black braid hanging down her back.

"I'm Andrew." Sitting in his chair, Andrew added in a whisper, "Is that boy's last name really Wonderful?"

Max grinned. "No. That's what his mom calls him. But he's not wonderful at all. He's the biggest pain in the whole school. In fact, he's the biggest pain in the whole city."

"He should get a medal," Casey said. "It takes a lot of effort to be the biggest pain out of one hundred and seventy thousand people. Now, let's work."

Andrew, Max, and Casey made a good team. When they disagreed about identifications, they didn't argue like some of the other teams were doing. They did more research until they figured it out. When Max was wrong and Andrew was right, Max offered his fist. "No hurt feelings. Gentleman's fist-bump?" They bumped their fists together.

"What if I'm right and one of you is wrong?" Casey said. "It's not a gentleman's fist-bump. It's not a lady's fist-bump either."

"Do girls fist-bump?" Max asked.

"We absolutely do," Casey said.

"How about a scientist's fist-bump?" Andrew suggested. They used the scientist's fist-bump after that. Professor Beek stopped by to glance over their papers and said it didn't look like they needed any of his help. Andrew was pleased. That meant they were getting everything right. Then the professor went over to Wally and asked him to join a group. Wally refused, saying that other kids just slowed him down.

Still, Andrew's team finished before anyone else in the room. Casey handed in their worksheets as Andrew and Max carried the shoeboxes to the teacher's table. Professor Beek wasn't up there. He was helping another group with a difficult identification.

Wally Wonderful got up to sharpen his pencil. Andrew saw him looking slyly at kids' papers while he did it.

The ooze was hanging from the grate. After Andrew put down the shoebox, he tapped on the glass. A ripple ran through the blob of goo. It dropped to the bottom of the bowl and splattered there. Slowly, it gathered itself back together.

"Was Professor Beek telling the truth about what it eats?" Andrew asked.

"Yeah," Max said. "I know the girl who lost all three of her cell phones."

The ooze slid up the side of the bowl. Andrew would have to check every morning to make sure his cell phone was turned off. Although he wanted to watch the ooze eat a phone, Mom and Dad weren't going to buy him another one if he lost his for such a stupid reason.

"Don't look so worried," Max said. "If you forget just one time, he won't drop your phone in there. Everyone is allowed to make a mistake. But if you keep forgetting, or if he catches you playing games or texting, that's when you can kiss your cell goodbye."

"I wonder what would happen if the ooze got out," Andrew said.

"I think everyone would have to grab all of their tech and run for it," Max said. That made Andrew laugh. He imagined thousands of hysterical people holding phones, laptops, and televisions while fleeing down the street as a small, glowing blob slid after them.

When class ended, Andrew left the room happily. Max and Casey waved and crossed the grass to waiting cars. Also going to a car was Wally Wonderful, who bumped into little kids left and right rather than walk around them.

He was a jerk, a cheating jerk. But Andrew could deal with one predator. One rounded down to nothing.

Brad was standing with a small group of kids beneath the school tree. He saw Andrew and ran over. "I don't want to go to the babysitter's house! Why can't I go home with you?"

"You're not old enough," Andrew said. "You'll have a good time over there. All you'll do is play and then Mom will bring you home."

"But some of those kids are *weird*."

They looked like regular kids to Andrew. Two were giggling and talking. Two were making faces at each other.

The last two were those strange sisters from the porch. Sitting beside the trunk, they were doing homework. They'd seemed weird to Andrew the day before, but they hadn't been mean. "Go back there, Brad."

"All they do at that lady's house is read and

play little kid games, they said! Like peek-a-boo and puzzles with the babies!" Brad cried.

"I can't take you." Andrew shifted his backpack. The colorful van was coming down the block. It had to go very slowly with all of the traffic.

Seeing the van, Brad turned red from anger. "Come on! I don't want to do dumb stuff over there. What kind of brother are you?"

Walking Brad back to the tree, Andrew said goodbye. To his back, Brad yelled, "I hate you!"

Andrew didn't answer. He wished he had a brother who wasn't angry all the time. The older Brad got, the angrier he became.

When Andrew got home, Shaggles was excited to see him. Jumping up and down at the back door, he barked. Andrew let him in. Then he turned his phone on and sent a text to Mom.

He had the whole house to himself. Well,

himself and Shaggles. They sat on the sofa together. Andrew ate a sandwich and read an article that Professor Beek had given out as homework. After that, it was television time.

"We're just two men alone at home," Andrew said to Shaggles. The dog wagged his tail in agreement, and put his head down to take a nap.

Three minutes before two o'clock, Andrew turned off the TV. He took his plate to the kitchen and put it in the dishwasher. Then he carried his backpack upstairs to his room. If he left a mess, Mom might decide he couldn't stay home alone.

As Andrew placed his backpack on his desk, Mom's car turned into the driveway. He watched her get out. Walking across the street to the babysitter's house, she knocked on the door.

The curtains fluttered furiously in the turret room.

No one answered. Mom knocked again.

A whole minute passed by. Just as Mom was raising her hand to knock a third time, the door opened and she went inside. Only seconds later, she came out with Brad. They crossed the street to home.

Andrew ran downstairs and opened the door. "Hi, Mom."

"Hi, honey," Mom said. "Brad, are you hungry? Do you want a snack?"

"Yes, please," Brad said.

Please? Brad had said please? Andrew stared at his little brother. Brad had to be reminded to say please each and every time.

"Once you've eaten, you can read a chapter of your book to me," Mom said. "Then you can watch cartoons."

"Okay," Brad said. "Hi, Andrew."

"Uhhh . . . hi," Andrew said. Brad usually held grudges for a lot longer than two hours. Also, he usually whined about having to do his homework.

Mom went into the kitchen to make the

snack. Andrew followed her in and said, "Why did it take so long for the babysitter to answer the door?"

"She was in another room dealing with a dirty diaper. I couldn't hear her calling for me to just come in," Mom said. "Nine kids! Nine kids she was taking care of when I got there. But they were playing so nicely and quietly, and some had their noses in books. She's got the golden touch with children."

Mom's cell phone rang. "I've got to take this call. Will you finish making this for me?"

She took the phone into the dining room. Andrew smeared peanut butter over the bread and pressed the slices together. Then he turned and jumped.

Brad was standing right behind him. Smiling.

"You scared me!" Andrew said.

"I'm sorry," Brad said.

That was just as weird as hearing *please* from him. Brad didn't apologize for anything unless Mom or Dad forced him. And it was rarely sincere.

Andrew handed over the plate. "Here's your snack."

"Thank you." Brad sat down at the kitchen table and picked up his sandwich.

He didn't glare at Andrew for not taking him home.

He didn't rip off the crusts in disgust.

He didn't complain that he had to do homework to earn his TV time.

He just ate. And smiled.

# CHAPTER FOUR

"**ARE** you feeling okay, Brad?" Mom asked the next morning. She put her hand on Brad's forehead to check his temperature.

"I feel fine," Brad said.

Andrew tied his shoelaces. He didn't think his brother looked fine. Brad always went at a snail's pace in the morning and made everybody late. He didn't want to brush his teeth. He couldn't find his backpack. He chewed every bite of his breakfast thirty times and swallowed in slow motion.

But today, Brad was ready before Andrew

was. His hair was combed. His shirt was tucked in. He was even wearing clean socks.

"No sore throat?" Mom said. "No stuffy nose? No tummy ache? You're so quiet."

"I'm practicing my spelling words in my head," Brad said. "Dragon, d-r-a-g-o-n."

"Good job!" Mom said in surprise.

On the walk to school, Andrew said, "What's wrong with you? Really? Why are you acting like this?"

"Acting like what?" Brad asked.

Andrew couldn't figure out how to say it. Finally, he said, "You know, *good.*"

"I like being good," Brad said. "Knight, k-n-i-g-h-t. That one is tricky, because it sounds just like night, n-i-g-h-t. Mrs. Myers says if you hear those words without context, you can't know which one it is. We have to listen very carefully to the sentence she says during our practice test so we know which one to spell."

"That's right," Andrew said, confused. This was some alien brother beside him.

"Right, r-i-g-h-t. Write, w-r-i-t-e." Brad laughed like that was hilarious. They crossed the street and he said, "I like those pumpkins. Do you?" He smiled at someone's yard. Dozens of little pumpkins were stacked into a pyramid in a wheelbarrow.

"You thought they were spooky just a few days ago!" Andrew cried. "Have you gone crazy? What happened?"

"I changed my mind. Now I like them."

Andrew opened his mouth to say that Brad was too stubborn to change his mind about anything, but then he snapped it shut. This was weird. This was *very* weird. But why was Andrew picking a fight the one time that Brad was in a good mood? Just yesterday, Andrew had wished for a brother who wasn't angry all the time.

When they got to school, Brad went to his classroom while chanting his spelling words. Andrew turned to Room 4.

Someone bumped into him, almost

knocking him down. "Hey, watch it!" Andrew exclaimed.

It was Wally Wonderful. "*You* watch it, Bigfoot."

Wally had walked into Andrew, not the other way around. "Maybe you need glasses," Andrew said angrily. "Big, thick ones."

"Maybe you need some fists to your face," Wally snapped. "Big, thick ones."

A shadow fell over them. Holding a shoebox, Professor Beek said, "Is there a problem, boys?"

Andrew didn't want to get in trouble on the second day of school. "No problem, Professor."

"He's got the problem," Wally said, and walked away.

From Professor Beek's expression, Andrew had the feeling that the teacher had seen the whole thing. "What's in the shoebox, Professor? Do you have more minerals for us to identify?"

"No," Professor Beek said. They headed

for Room 4 together. "I noticed the ooze hanging from the grate a lot yesterday. Usually it does that when it's getting hungry. I brought it some cell phones."

"Where did you get them?"

"Oh, I went to the theater last night. It's very rude for people to use cell phones when a movie is playing. The light bothers everyone. So I took them away." He opened the lid to show Andrew a collection of cell phones. "There are still ten minutes to the bell. Would you like to come in with me and feed it while I set up for the day?"

*Would* he? "Yes!" Andrew said.

Professor Beek looked at the other students who had come early. There was only Wally Wonderful and Max, who stood far apart from each another. "Perhaps you'd like to select a friend to feed the ooze with you, Andrew?"

Both Wally and Max got excited. But there was only one of those two that Andrew would ever choose. "Max! Let's do this!"

Professor Beek unlocked the door and the three of them went inside. "Now remember," he said, "you have to shake the ooze off the grate first. It should be all the way at the bottom of the bowl before you drop in the cell phone. And give it the biggest phone in the box. It hasn't had anything to munch on since April."

The professor gave the shoebox to Andrew and went to the cupboards. Max cleared a space beside the bowl and Andrew dumped out the phones.

The ooze was hanging from the grate. It didn't have eyes, but it seemed to sense a meal. Moving to the side of the bowl closest to the phones, it clung there almost hopefully.

Max lined up the five phones. One was very old and small, three were exactly the same size, and the last one was huge. Max pushed the biggest one to Andrew as the ooze slid up to the grate.

"You shake it off and whisk away the

grate," Andrew said. "Then I'll drop in the phone and you can slam the top back on."

Max took hold of the grate and shook it. The ooze clung on. "Poor little guy. It's starving," Max said. Shaking the grate harder, he made the ooze fall to the bottom. It hit with a loud splat, and rapidly began to come together.

"Quick! Quick!" Andrew said.

Max yanked away the grate and Andrew dropped in the big cell phone. It bounced off the bottom of the bowl and hit the side. Then it bounced again and landed squarely on top of the ooze. Max put the grate back on and huddled down beside Andrew to watch.

The glowing, grayish-green ooze quivered. Andrew thought that it was surprised to find a phone suddenly sitting upon itself.

"Look at *that*," Max said in amazement.

The phone was sinking into the ooze bit by bit. Down and down and down it went, goo rising up on all four sides. When it could sink no further, the ooze collapsed over the phone and rippled.

The boys squinted at the bowl. The cell phone was almost invisible within the center of the blob. The glowing got brighter and brighter, until it was so bright that Andrew and Max had to cover their eyes. "Is this normal, professor?" Max said in a raised voice.

"Totally normal!" Professor Beek called from elsewhere in the classroom.

When they peeked between their fingers, the glowing had dimmed to its regular level. The ooze rolled around the bottom of the bowl and slid up the side to the grate. "Do you see the phone?" Andrew asked.

Max shook his head. The ooze hung from the top and dropped all on its own. It splattered into a thin layer of goo on the bottom. The phone was gone. There wasn't a scrap of it left anywhere.

"Here's an interesting question that keeps me up at night," Professor Beek said, coming over to look as the ooze gathered up to its blob shape. "Is it alive?"

"It moves," Max said. "But so does a robot, and a robot isn't alive."

"Does it get bigger?" Andrew asked. "Living things get bigger."

"No, it always stays that size," the professor said. "It certainly responds to its environment, which is a characteristic of life. Yet it does not grow, nor does it make more of itself, or perhaps it has just not done those things yet. I don't believe it breathes. So it does not meet all the criteria for life, as far as we know, but what is it?"

"It's a mystery of science," Max said.

"Have you ever seen one of these before?" Andrew asked.

"I am afraid not," the professor said. "Only here. It is just another of the many mysteries of Chills Hills. Luckily, this is a harmless one."

"There are more mysteries?"

"Mysteries upon mysteries upon

mysteries," the professor said, and opened the door to let the rest of the students in.

# CHAPTER FIVE

"**HE** lives in a huge house on Acorn Drive," Casey said. "*Huge*. There's a pool in back. And he has two bedrooms all to himself."

It was Friday, and Wally Wonderful had gotten sent to the office. For once, the trouble had nothing to do with Andrew. The lone predator of Room 4 had knocked over another group's experiment on purpose when they wouldn't let him copy off their worksheets.

All done with their work, Andrew, Casey, and Max were talking quietly at their table in the back. "Two bedrooms?" Andrew asked. "What does he do with the second?"

"It was like a toy store," Casey said. "Wall to wall. I went to his eighth birthday party there and saw it for myself. The coolest toys, computers and a drum set, and he didn't allow us to play with anything. He screamed his head off when someone hit the cymbal. He hates for people to touch his stuff. Everyone was invited to the party, not just his class but the whole *grade*. Each grade has three classes at this school, so it was seventy-five kids. There were bouncy houses and cotton candy machines and clowns making balloon animals and everything. And four cakes! Three were giant, plain old sheet cakes for us, but the fourth was fancy and for Wally to have all to himself."

"Did you go to that party?" Andrew asked Max.

Max nodded. "His cake said Wally Wonderful on it. No lie."

"But the worst was when he was opening his seventy-five presents," Casey said. "Most of them he called cheap or dumb and tossed to the side. It was so rude. Dad and I had picked out a neat Zip Wheelie car for him. Wally collected Zip Wheelies back then. He opened it up, said he already had that one, and shoved it back to me since he didn't want it. I've gotten invitations to his parties since then, but Dad says I don't have to go."

"I don't go to Wally's parties either now," Max said. "Most people don't anymore, especially after the year he stole all the goody bags. His parents think he's the greatest kid ever. The smartest, too. But he cheats on tests all the time, just waits until the teacher isn't looking and flat-out stares at your paper. *He* didn't earn those A's and B's he got last year. *I* did, and he swiped them for himself. I blocked my paper as much as I could, but he still found a way."

"And he takes lunches," Casey said. "If you

don't hide it in your desk, he'll swipe whatever he likes from it. He's mean to everyone and he talks back to teachers. And his mom buys him a present every day after school!"

"Every *day*?" Andrew exclaimed in disbelief.

"He brags about it," Max said. "It doesn't even matter if he got in trouble that day. His parents always blame the teacher for being mean to him, or us for bullying him when he bullies us. So he still gets his present. They'll go to the toy store or that Big Games downtown. I've seen them there. If *I* brought home a note from my teacher saying I'd stolen someone's lunch?" Max's eyes widened. "I'd be grounded for weeks. My mom *definitely* wouldn't be taking me out to buy me a new video game."

"All right, everybody!" Professor Beek called. "Put down your pens and pencils and go stretch your legs outside. I'll see you in twenty minutes and then why don't we blow something up before all of you go home for the weekend?"

Everyone cheered. The ooze rolled joyfully around its bowl. Eating the cell phone had given it a lot of energy. Sometimes it rolled so fast that it turned into a glowing blur.

All of the classes were having recess. The little kids were going down the slides and swinging on the monkey bars in the playground. The older ones were playing soccer on the field and basketball in the courts. Max went into the boys' restroom and a group of girls called for Casey.

Andrew saw Brad. He was sitting all by himself on a bench near the playground.

Brad hadn't argued once all week about brushing his teeth or doing his homework. He just did it without being asked. One afternoon, Andrew had pitched the baseball for him in the yard. Even though he missed it nine times out of ten, he didn't get mad. He only smiled and said cheerfully, "Better luck next time!"

It was like Brad had been swapped with Robot Brad. He was no longer alive but acting out a computer program. While it was nice to not be fighting with him, Andrew got a serious case of the creeps whenever he saw that empty smile. Mom and Dad had been concerned at first, but now they thought the move had been very good for him.

Shaggles, however, did not agree. Whenever Brad came near him, the dog tucked his tail between his legs and ran away.

All of the kids on the playground were having a great time. Andrew jogged over to the bench and sat down by his brother. "Did a teacher make you sit here because you got in trouble?"

"No," Brad said.

"Then why aren't you playing?"

"I like to watch," Brad said.

"Are you having a hard time making friends?"

"No."

Maybe he was just tired, Andrew thought. The kids in Reading 'n Racing had several recesses every day.

"Don't you want to go down the slide just once?" Andrew asked. "What about that big one that curves around? That looks like fun."

"It looks fun," Brad agreed, but he didn't get up.

Andrew tried again. "You like to swing. That one is free over there. You could jump off from way up high."

"That's against the rules," Brad said.

Of course it was against the rules, but everybody did it anyway. You just had to bide your time until the playground monitor wasn't looking. And since when did Brad care about the playground rules? He loved to jump off the swings.

Andrew pointed to the monkey bars. "I bet you can't skip two yet! Your tiny arms won't stretch that far."

Brad should have run over there at once to prove it. But he didn't say anything.

"Hey, Andrew! Andrew!" Max yelled from the edge of the field. "Come on! I've got a basketball! We can shoot hoops at the court over there."

"Hold on a second!" Andrew called back. "Brad, are the kids in your class not being nice to you? Is that why you're over here?"

"I just want to sit," Brad said.

It wasn't a crime to sit. But it didn't make any sense. The only part of school that Brad liked was recess.

"Okay," Andrew said. He got up and left Brad there.

As he passed the playground to reach Max, he saw a boy sitting on the pipe logs around the playground. He was five or six, and he was watching the kids play just like Brad was.

His hair was combed.

His shirt was tucked in.

His socks were clean and pulled up almost

to his knees.

Andrew stopped dead in his tracks to stare at the kid. Then he looked around. In the grass beyond the playground were those strange sisters. They were sitting next to one another without talking, their hands folded in their laps. And there was another kid in the far corner! Sitting on a stump, she didn't react when two kids ran by and kicked up sand on her legs.

And there was Brad on the bench in the distance, doing nothing.

How bizarre. It made Andrew nervous.

"Go *play*!" he shouted to Brad.

His voice was so loud that it rang out over the school. The normal kids on the slides and swings paid no attention. The two chasing each other looked over to Andrew. One shouted, "We *are* playing!"

"Hurry up, Andrew!" Max called.

But Andrew was frozen in place. Because the robot kids all turned their heads at the same time to him, and smiled identical smiles.

# CHAPTER SIX

**ANDREW** couldn't get those five empty, creepy smiles out of his head. It was all he thought about during Professor Beek's explosion.

Someone was making Brad act like this. That was the only explanation. Maybe his Reading 'n Racing class had a mean teacher, or a lot of mean students. Or there could be mean kids at the babysitter's house. Maybe someone had scared Brad into thinking he had to be good all the time. Or else.

Instead of walking home as soon as the bell

rang, Andrew went to the front of the school and hid around the corner to spy. There was Brad at the tree with a group of kids. The sisters were doing their homework in the grass. Three more were doing dance moves. Brad stared out to the cars pulling up to the curb.

Nobody was teasing him. The other kids didn't even look at him.

The colorful van came down the road. It paused as a spot opened up at the curb, and slid in smoothly to take it. Rolling down the passenger side window, the woman in the driver's seat yelled merrily, "Come on, kids!"

Mrs. Dritch was old, but not as old as Professor Beek. Her black hair was up in a bun and she had a friendly smile. Through a back window, Andrew saw a car seat with a baby in it.

The kids at the tree picked up their things and went to the van. Three were still dancing along the way. They piled in and Mrs. Dritch said, "Put on your seatbelts, everybody!"

She turned on kids' music and rolled up the window. The van pulled away from the curb and drove to the corner, where it stopped at the red light.

Andrew came out of his hiding place once the van was gone. There had been nothing weird about any of that. Nothing at all. To tell the truth, it had been pretty boring to watch.

But something was wrong. He was sure of it.

He walked home, deep in thought. After sending Mom a text, he let in Shaggles and made a sandwich. Upstairs, he ate it while he sat by the window. The van was parked in the driveway.

His binoculars! Most of Andrew's things were unpacked, but he didn't find them in his closet or desk drawer. Going to the last two boxes in the corner, he searched through them. At the very bottom of the second box were his binoculars.

Andrew put the strap around his neck and looked through them to Mrs. Dritch's house. He started at the top with the turret room. The curtains were still. On the second floor, trees blocked many of the windows. But he could see part of the way into one. It was a bathroom.

Normal. Boring.

It was hard to see into any of the rooms on the first floor except the living room. The sun was reflecting off the glass, and all Andrew could make out was a stretch of green carpet and a line of backpacks on hooks. There were no kids.

Where was everybody? He had seen her drive away with a loaded van of kids.

Andrew needed to get a closer look, and it had to be now. It was already one o'clock. If Mom came home a little early from work and he wasn't there . . . Hurrying down the stairs, he let himself out the door. He ran to the tree in his front yard and concealed himself behind the thick trunk.

He looked through his binoculars again. It was just a house like every other house on the block, only with a turret and more foliage. He moved the binoculars all around, from the turret room to the jack-o'-lanterns beneath the shaggy trees. Mrs. Dritch's driveway was lined with tall, thin hedges and a rock wall. Beyond the wall was an alley.

Andrew hesitated. He was supposed to be inside, not spying on a perfectly normal house.

But this would only take a few minutes. Just a peek or two and he would go back in to do his homework. Mom would never know that he'd been outside.

He ran across the street and into the alley, his heart pounding. The wall was tall, and the hedges were even taller. They blocked his view of the house completely. Even when he backed up, he couldn't see anything but a hint of the roof.

No voices. With so many kids over there, why wasn't he hearing voices? No shouts, no screams, no cries, no laughter.

Nothing.

He crept down the alley. It ran along Mrs. Dritch's house and the house behind hers. After that, it ended at a street. Nobody was in the alley but Andrew.

When he was almost at the end of Mrs. Dritch's property, he spotted a gap in the hedges. Checking left and right first, he jumped up and grabbed the top of the wall to pull himself up.

The ledge was narrow, nearly too narrow to crouch upon. Bending into an awkward position, he peered through the gap. A hedge was missing here, but the hedges on the other sides had grown leafy twigs over it. They gave Andrew cover.

The backyard was massive, and speckled with shadows from the trees. A few kids stood on the far end near box beds full of tomato plants and cucumber vines. Andrew lifted his binoculars to see what they were doing.

The kids who had been dancing beside the school tree were now picking dandelions. A boy brought one to his lips to blow it, and his companions shook their heads. He dropped it in a bucket instead. All three of them bent to the grass to pull weeds.

Closer to the house, the strange sisters were washing toys in a tub full of bubbles. One hunched over the tub and scrubbed hard at each toy before giving it to the other, who rinsed it off with the hose and put it on a towel to dry. They were baby toys, plastic rings and balls.

Nobody was talking. They were the quietest kids that Andrew had ever seen.

He turned at a squeaking sound. Coming around the far side of the house, Brad was pulling a red wagon on a small concrete area. In the wagon was the baby, who laughed in delight. Brad smiled at nothing as he pulled the baby around in a circle and vanished behind the house.

A minute went by. The squeaking returned and Andrew watched his brother make the same loop. The baby was the only child in the whole backyard making noise.

The back door opened. Mrs. Dritch came out and stood on the top step. The breeze fluttered her long gray shirt. Clapping her hands for attention, she called, "Time for a snack! Popcorn today!"

They didn't cheer, or even look excited.

The strange sisters left the toys, and the kids doing the weeding stopped as well. Brad picked up the baby and brought him to the steps, where Mrs. Dritch was passing out juice boxes and paper cups full of popcorn. She took the baby and carried him inside.

The kids sat on the steps with their snacks and ate silently. When they were done, they took their trash into the house. Finally there was only one boy left. He was the one who had wanted to blow the dandelion. Tipping the cup, he gobbled up the last pieces of his popcorn.

Mrs. Dritch reappeared as the boy tried to go inside. "Why don't you give me your trash, Shawn? I'll throw it away and you can dump that bucket of weeds in the green waste can. Leave the bucket over there when you're done."

Andrew thought the kid named Shawn looked a little afraid. But why? There was no reason to be afraid. Mrs. Dritch hadn't spoken to him in anger.

Shawn ran down the steps and over the grass to the bucket. Snatching the handle, he raced in Andrew's direction. Andrew stayed very still as the kid threw out the weeds. The lid of the trashcan fell down with a bang and the boy tore back to the steps.

"Let's have some homework time, shall we?" Mrs. Dritch asked pleasantly, stepping aside to let Shawn in. She looked over the yard.

Something clattered beneath Andrew, like the bucket had fallen over. Mrs. Dritch turned and stared right at him.

Andrew jerked away from the gap and lost his balance on the ledge. Falling off it, he landed with a thump in the alley. His heart was pounding even harder than before. He raced to the far end and swerved onto the sidewalk before looking back.

She wasn't coming after him. She probably hadn't even seen him through the leaves. But he ran all the way around the block until he was on their street, and sneaked home with his eye on her house. It wasn't until he was back in his bedroom that his heart stopped pounding so madly against his ribcage.

Was he being ridiculous? Or was there really something going on?

He looked out the window. All was still over there.

Too still.

# CHAPTER SEVEN

**IT** was Sunday night, and Andrew had to talk to Mom or Dad about this.

In his pocket was a folded up piece of paper with a list of the ways that Brad was different.

He didn't whine.

He didn't throw things.

He used his manners.

He took showers.

All of his toys were picked up.

He was ready for school on time.

He did his chores.

He ate his vegetables.

He talked like a robot.

The dog was scared of him.

After Brad went upstairs to get ready for bed, Andrew hunted through the house for his parents. Dad had taken Shaggles on a walk, and Mom was sitting on the sofa with her digital reader.

"Mom, I think there's a problem with Brad," Andrew said.

She closed her reader at once and said worriedly, "What is it?"

Suddenly, Andrew felt dumb about the list he'd made. "He's . . . acting strange, I guess."

Mom relaxed. "Honey, he's just growing up a little."

"He doesn't even try to fight with me about anything anymore."

"I would have thought you'd like that." Mom laughed. "Do you want him to fight with you?"

"No, but . . ."

Something was strange about the

babysitter, but he had no evidence. What could he say? Mrs. Dritch had made them pick weeds, wash toys, and play with the baby, and she gave them popcorn for a snack. None of that was spooky or threatening. For all Andrew knew, the kids could have volunteered to do those things in the yard. They could have been playing a game to see who could be quiet the longest. And Andrew shouldn't have been over there to see any of it in the first place.

"I know it's been rough on you," Mom said. "Having Brad always spoiling for a fight. But look at it from his perspective. He thinks you're perfect. He thinks you're the most amazing person, and he's jealous of you."

Andrew didn't believe that. "He doesn't think I'm amazing. He hates me. And why would he be jealous?"

"You get such good grades in school. You play a wonderful game of baseball. He wants to keep up, but he can't. Everybody in this world has different strengths. Instead of searching for his own strengths, he's desperate to be strong in the exact same ways you are. It makes him angry when he falls short."

"What are his strengths?"

"Remember how well he sang in his music performances back in kindergarten and first grade? He has a real talent for music. But he didn't want to keep doing that since *you* weren't. That's what I mean, Andrew. In his mind, you're incredible. He wishes he could be incredible, too."

This still didn't explain how different Brad was now from the way he was before they moved. "But it happened so fast, Mom. It was like he went to the babysitter one day and *changed*. He shouldn't go back there. I can bring him home with me and watch him until you get here."

"Andrew, she's a very nice woman!" Mom said.

"Are you sure?"

"Yes! You're going to see it for yourself tomorrow."

Shocked, Andrew said, "What? Mom! You're sending me to the *babysitter*?"

"Just for tomorrow. We've got the pest guys coming in the morning to spray the backyard, and they recommended we stay away from the house until mid-afternoon. Dad is taking Shaggles to a doggie daycare for the day. I already talked to Mrs. Dritch about you coming. She understands that you're a little old for babysitting and won't need anything from her. You can just sit on the front porch there or in the living room and do your homework."

A million arguments popped into Andrew's mind. Then he realized that this was an opportunity. He could see the inside of Mrs. Dritch's house. There had to be a reason for all of this in there.

When he woke up the next morning, he

found Brad in his room. "What are you doing?" Andrew asked.

"I'm cleaning up," Brad said, lining up Andrew's shoes in the closet. "I like to clean."

"No, you don't!" Andrew exploded. This was too much. "Get out of here!"

They didn't speak to one another on the walk to school. Andrew could barely bring himself to look at that robot smile and vacant eyes. Like Brad had checked out, and no one was home. They parted at the jack-o'-lanterns outside the school, Andrew walking backwards to see his brother.

A teacher was standing in the open doorway to Brad's room. Sitting on the walkway were lots of kids trading dragon cards. Ignoring them, Brad went to the teacher and said, "Good morning, Mrs. Myers! It's a nice day!"

"Well, good morning, Mr. Bradley Calistoga!" the teacher said with a smile. "I'll let you guys into the room in just a minute."

"Teacher's pet," scoffed a boy with two fistfuls of dragon cards. Without reacting, Brad sat down and took out his spelling words to review them.

The morning passed slowly. It was hard for Andrew to keep his mind on science when he wanted to be investigating Mrs. Dritch. Even the ooze was not fun to watch, but that could have been because it was splattered along the bottom of the bowl and not moving much. Professor Beek said that was normal behavior, although he had no idea why the ooze did it. His best guess was that this was how it slept.

"You should jam a fork into it super hard," Wally said with a nasty grin. "Wake it up."

"I shall remember your advice," Professor Beek said solemnly, "should *you* ever fall asleep in my class and need waking up."

Andrew hoped when school started up in the fall that he was not in the same class as Wally Wonderful. Or if he was, that at least Max was there to share in Wally's awfulness with him.

The bell finally rang and he said goodbye to Max and Casey. The kids going to the babysitter had already gathered under the school tree. Andrew joined them in embarrassment. He was a head taller than everybody else.

"Who are you?" Shawn asked.

"I'm Andrew, Brad's brother," Andrew said. "What are all of your names?"

"I'm Shawn, and those girls are Daisy and Linny." Shawn pointed to the strange sisters. As always, they were doing their homework. His finger shifted to another girl and a boy on the far side of the tree. "That's Veronica and Grant."

Andrew recognized Grant from last week. He had never seen Veronica until now. She had pigtails and an angry face. Dropping her backpack, she glared at the grass.

Mrs. Dritch pulled up at the curb and waved. All of them went to the van, Veronica kicking her backpack the entire way. There were two seats in the trunk, which Daisy and Linny took. Brad, Grant, and Shawn sat in the back row. The baby laughed in his car seat in the row ahead of that.

"Why don't you sit in the front, Andrew?" Mrs. Dritch said. Andrew would have rather sat in the back, but he opened the passenger side door.

Veronica gave her backpack another kick. It hit the side of the van.

"Pick it up and climb in!" Mrs. Dritch said cheerfully.

Veronica hovered at the door. "I don't want to go with you. My *dad* is supposed to get me today. I'm supposed to be at his house this week."

"I'm sorry that he couldn't be here," Mrs. Dritch said. "Let's go!"

"I don't want to!"

Andrew looked behind him. Grant and Shawn had worried expressions. Brad was staring out the window, and the strange sisters did the same out the back.

Mrs. Dritch did not get upset. Smiling, she said to Veronica, "All right, this is your first warning."

Veronica's bottom lip poked out. Lifting her backpack, she climbed into the van. Mrs. Dritch hit a button and the door rolled shut. "Seatbelts!"

They clicked all over the van. She drove down the street and stopped at the light. "Are you enjoying your science class, Andrew?"

Nervously, Andrew said, "Yeah. We do cool stuff."

"How wonderful. Look at that grumpy face!" Mrs. Dritch had glanced through the rearview mirror to Veronica. "I'll put on music. That will make you feel better."

They arrived at the house within three minutes. Everybody piled out, Veronica still in a bad mood. Swinging the baby onto her hip, Mrs. Dritch said, "It's special movie day!

Everybody into the living room!"

Andrew walked into a very ordinary living room. The little kids hung up their backpacks on the hooks and went to a coat closet, where they pulled out a stack of small chairs. Arranging them around the television, they sat down.

As Andrew stood there uncertainly, Mrs. Dritch said, "Your mother told me that you'd probably like to study on the porch. That's quite all right. It takes a lot of work to earn those A's!"

"May I study on the sofa?" Andrew said. He had to observe this place, and he couldn't do it from the porch.

"Of course you can, as long as the sound doesn't disturb you." Mrs. Dritch put the baby in a swing and slid a DVD into the player. An animated movie began.

"This is a stupid movie!" Veronica spat.

"And this is your second warning," Mrs. Dritch said softly. Shawn and Grant paled and

**77**

stared at one another. Veronica settled down.

An hour later, Andrew was forced to conclude that he had been wrong. Nothing odd was going on here. This was just a regular old babysitter and a regular old house. The kids watched the movie while Mrs. Dritch cleaned the kitchen.

Yet not all of the kids were regular. Brad, Daisy, and Linny stared at the screen without squirming or talking. Even when they laughed at a joke, it was only after the rest of the kids started laughing. On the other hand, Shawn, Grant, and Veronica were totally regular. Shawn was kicking his foot absent-mindedly against his chair leg, and Grant cracked his knuckles every five minutes.

Arms folded across her chest, Veronica watched the movie sourly. "Stop doing that," she complained when Grant cracked his knuckles again.

"I have to," Grant said. "If I don't, my knuckles hurt."

"They hurt because you crack them, dummy!" Veronica shouted.

"Shhh, you'll get a third warning!" Shawn whispered.

A chill fell over the room.

Veronica's loud voice had brought Mrs. Dritch to the doorway. "Do we need to go upstairs, Veronica?" she asked sweetly.

Veronica's cheeks turned red and her eyebrows lowered. She looked like she was about to explode into a temper tantrum.

"It's okay," Grant said in fright. "I didn't mean to bother her. I won't crack them anymore."

"Do we need to go upstairs?" Mrs. Dritch repeated.

The only sound in the room was from the television. Brad and the strange sisters didn't turn around in their chairs to see what was going on.

Mrs. Dritch stared at Veronica, and Veronica stared at Mrs. Dritch. The air was heavy around Andrew, the way it felt when a storm was about to break. For no reason he could name, he was filled with fear.

Veronica broke the stare first. "No," she said meekly. "I'm sorry. I shouldn't have yelled."

Mrs. Dritch returned to the kitchen. Veronica turned back to the movie and didn't say another word.

And Andrew stayed on the sofa, afraid.

# CHAPTER EIGHT

"**MAY** I ask you something?" Andrew said.

School was over for the day, but Andrew had lingered in the classroom as everyone left. Professor Beek was stacking up papers on his desk in the corner while the ooze spun in place at the bottom of the bowl.

"I have a staff meeting in the office in five minutes," Professor Beek said. "But if it's a quick question, then go ahead and ask. Is it about the homework?"

"No. It's about something you said last week." Andrew shrugged like it wasn't all that important. "We were talking about the ooze, and you said it's a mystery. You said Chills Hills is full of mysteries. I was just wondering because . . . there weren't really any mysteries in the city where I used to live. Everything was normal. But here . . . here it's not quite the same."

"Chills Hills," Professor Beek said, shaking his head as he stuffed the papers into a file. "It's not quite the same, that's true. Andrew, do you know the meaning of the word affront?"

"No, but I've heard it before."

"When 'affront' is used as a noun, it indicates something that has caused offense.

Insult. Indignity. Chills Hills is an affront to the scientific mind."

"How so, Professor?"

"If someone told us that the reason grass is green is because trillions of tiny fairies paint our lawns every night, would we believe it?"

"No."

"No!" Professor Beek cried. "Have any of us ever seen armies of fairies flying about with little cans of paint and brushes? Is there any proof that that is actually why grass is green? We look to science for explanations of what we do not understand. We do experiments until we get an answer, an answer that can be reached over and over again in identical circumstances. But I have found that what is a scientific truth everywhere else in the world is not necessarily true within this lovely city of ours. Come with me."

They walked outside. After the professor locked the door to Room 4, they started for the office. All of the kids had already been picked up, so the hallway and lawn were empty.

"The student who created the ooze was mixing chemicals at random that she had taken without permission from my cupboard," Professor Beek said. "I know all the chemicals she stole that day, the approximate amounts she used, and the order in which she used them. None of that can account for the ooze that slid out of the beaker. In my laboratory at home, I have attempted countless times to duplicate what she did. I can't, Andrew. How is that

**84**

possible?"

"I don't know," Andrew said.

"I could tell you a dozen stories like that, if I had the time. But the conclusion to each tale is the same: this city does not stand on the same footing as the rest of the world. And since we have absolutely no understanding of what *type* of footing it is that lies beneath our feet, we must always proceed with caution."

"So chemicals don't do here what they would do out there," Andrew said.

"Not always. Often enough they do, often enough so that there is still a point to the teaching of science. But now and then, they do not, and that is a mystery I may never solve."

"What about people?"

"What about them?"

"Do people change here?" Andrew asked. "Could somebody be one person out there, yet another when they come to Chills Hills?"

They stopped at the door to the office. Professor Beek looked thoughtful. "I cannot say. It is not something that I have seen for myself."

Andrew was disappointed.

"But my experience is not everyone's experience. How could it be? We are not the same, and we see different things. I have found that it is wise to look through the eyes of others when studying the phenomena of this city," Professor Beek said. "Just because I have not seen something personally does not mean that it does not exist. As to your specific concern, perhaps a person *could* change. What are our bodies made of if not chemicals? We are water and protein and fat, vitamins and DNA, and gases both fortunate and unfortunate. Yes, some very unfortunate gas indeed. Does this answer your question?"

"Sort of." Andrew blurted, "Does it scare you?"

Professor Beek put his hand on the doorknob. He looked past Andrew to the jack-o'-lanterns. "At times. To be without the rules that should govern us . . . it has disturbed me over the years. Is something troubling you, Andrew?"

Andrew could not bring himself to tell the professor about Mrs. Dritch when all he had was a creepy feeling. "No. I was just curious."

"A good trait in any scientist. Hold onto it.

Now, if you will excuse me." He opened the door.

"Have you ever wondered why people here put out pumpkins so early?" Andrew asked quickly.

"I have wondered, and never do I receive a satisfactory answer. I am forced to quote myself: mysteries upon mysteries upon mysteries," Professor Beek said, and went inside.

# CHAPTER NINE

"**SO**, what's the matter?" Max asked. On a break, they were walking around the field together. "Sorry I couldn't call you back yesterday. My mom had me cleaning out the pantry."

"No problem," Andrew said. "It's not that important. I just wanted to know . . . well, because I'm new here . . . has anything weird ever happened to you?"

Andrew had been dreading for hours that Max was going to give him an odd look as an answer.

Max looked wary. "What do you mean?"

"It's hard to explain. Truthfully, explaining it is going to make you think that *I'm* weird."

Max pulled him away from a group of kids and said in a low voice, "Do you have a ghost in your house?"

That was not what Andrew had expected Max to say. "No. Is that common around here?"

Max did not reply. He just looked away.

"Please, I'm not making fun of you," Andrew said. "Something a little strange is going on in my family, and it didn't start until we moved here. Why did you think it might be a ghost? Do you have one at your house?"

"No," Max said.

They sat down at a picnic table and Max hesitated. Then he spoke. "It's Chills Hills to a lot of people. Just a regular old place with a funny name. Kids go to school, grownups go to work, the stores open in the morning and close at night. You sit in traffic. You get the mail. You watch TV. It's like anywhere else, any other city in the world. Just with a few more pumpkins. Understand?"

"Like where I lived before," Andrew said.

"Yeah. But it has another face, a darker face. That's Chillz Hillz. Hear the difference?"

Andrew nodded. The difference wasn't just in the changed letters. There was something dangerous about the way Max said it. Something that made a shiver run up Andrew's spine.

"That's how we think of the city's other side," Max said. "Kids mostly, and some grownups who see things like we do. Chillz Hillz is not the same as Chills Hills, not at all. You haven't ever lived in a place like this."

Max motioned to a girl playing soccer. "There's a room in her house that her family doesn't dare to go in. You don't see anything if you do. You don't hear anything either. But you *feel* it, creeping up behind you. You're one hundred percent positive that it's about to jump on your back and dig in its claws. And then you whirl around and nothing's there, nothing but empty air . . . but you feel it creeping up on you from the other direction now. So they just don't use that room, and they keep the door locked."

"Have you seen it for yourself?"

"No, I've never been to her place. But she's not a liar, Andrew. She shakes when she talks about it. That room scares her half to death." Max pointed to a boy on the basketball court. "That's Graham over there, the one dribbling two balls. It's in the closets in his house. The doors open all by themselves. If he blocks one with a chair, something pounds on the other side. It gets louder and louder until he takes the chair away. Then the door swings open."

"But nothing comes out?" Andrew said, alarmed.

"Nothing comes out. Nothing goes in. Nothing that he can see. His parents just say it's an old house with a cracked foundation, so everything is off balance and there's no reason to worry. Maybe that explains why the doors open, but *who's knocking?*"

It was a very hot day, yet Andrew was still shivering. "Anybody else?"

"I'm sure there are, but I don't know a lot of those little kids. But you have to be careful what you say, and where you say it. A lot of grownups don't like to hear about ghosts and things like that, especially the ones who see this place as Chills Hills and nothing else. They'll think you want attention, or that you've got something wrong up here and need help."

Max tapped his forehead three times. "It's not just houses either. There was the haunted bicycle back in fourth grade."

He gave Andrew another wary look. Andrew said, "I'm not laughing."

"Some people do. But it wasn't a joke. Teddy got the bike for Christmas that year. Brand new, a blue speed racer. Every time he rode it, he crashed. And Teddy is no beginner.

He's been riding bikes forever. He wants to ride professionally one day, race all over the world. He can ride better and faster than anyone I've ever met. But he said that bike just kept steering *itself* into trashcans and parked cars. He'd get all banged up. It scared him how the bike had a mind of its own. A mind with a mean streak. After a while, he didn't want it anymore. Denny offered him twenty bucks for it. The bike still looked new, and Denny didn't believe it was haunted. The first time he rode it, he broke his leg."

*"How?"*

"He was riding along and the bicycle suddenly turned down a steep hill and sped up. He hit the brakes and it didn't slow. It went faster and faster, even flying past cars, until it jerked and rode into a tree. Denny flew twenty feet through the air and landed in some guy's yard. He was in a cast for ages. And the bike was totally fine! There wasn't a scratch on it anywhere."

A teacher walked past them. Max waited until she was gone before he went on with his story. "After that, Denny didn't want the bike either. He said he'd pay someone to take it away. He was that scared of it. Kelly said she'd take the bike and twenty bucks. So then she had it. She wasn't sure if she believed it was haunted, but she didn't want to risk it. She parked the bike in her garage and spent the money. Nothing happened for a long time and she forgot it was even in there. Then one night, she heard a strange sound in the driveway. She looked out her window and there it was, going around and around in circles with nobody riding it! That was enough for her. She walked it away from her house in the morning and left it in front of a store. Someone stole it a couple of hours later. And then there was the ghoul can . . . but what's going on with you?"

After those stories, Andrew's story didn't seem all that weird. "If I tell you, do you promise not to laugh?"

"I promise. I'll believe you, whatever it is. Nothing is too weird for Chillz Hillz. Haunted garage? Spooky shoes? Ghoul can?"

"It's my little brother. I don't know what happened exactly. He goes to a babysitter after school. She lives across the street from us. It's just for two hours until our mom is done with work. But the first day he went over there . . . he came back as someone else."

"Is the babysitter's last name Dritch?" Max asked.

Shocked, Andrew exclaimed, "Yes! YES! How did you know?"

"Mrs. Dritch babysits for loads of kids at this school since she lives so close by. She was even my babysitter for a few weeks when I was in second grade. Usually my gramma gets me, but she was having surgery on her knee so I went to Mrs. Dritch's house. All the parents love her. But I didn't like it there."

"Why?"

"You have to be quiet. She likes it very quiet, especially when she takes a catnap in her recliner."

Andrew had thought that was strange the day he was over there. For half an hour, the babysitter took a nap while the kids did their homework and the baby rested in a crib. It had been so weird to be in the same room with her sleeping that Andrew had gone out to the porch.

"You have to do whatever she says," Max said. "You wash her car, feed the babies, or watch a cartoon even if you've seen it a hundred times. You eat whatever snack she gives you, even if it's something you hate. You can't argue or refuse. Or else she takes you upstairs."

"What happens upstairs?"

"I don't know. I just kept my head down and stayed quiet like she wanted. She never got mad at anyone, but she still freaked me out. But I saw her take Allen up there. That was my last day at her house. Back then, Allen was always in trouble at school. He got sent to the principal every week for goofing off in class, talking and bothering people. His grades were horrible. He didn't want to do his homework when Mrs. Dritch said it was study time. She took her nap while we worked at the dining room table. Allen was messing around next to me, flicking rubber bands at all of us, doodling on his paper, singing and making fart sounds."

Max looked down to the ground and squeezed his hands together. Just the memory of that day scared him. "He wouldn't stop. We all whispered for him to knock it off, but he didn't. He kept waking up Mrs. Dritch in the living room. She came in to give him a warning each time and fell back asleep in her chair. But he'd only be quiet for a couple of minutes, and then . . ."

Max blew a loud, rattling raspberry. "The third time he woke her up, she got his arm and took him upstairs. She said he needed a talking-to. But I didn't hear a thing from up there, not a peep. Then they came back down. Allen sat at the table and did his homework. No more rubber bands, no doodles or farts, and he's been like that ever since. He gets on the honor roll every quarter. All of the Dritch kids are on the honor roll. I was so glad when my gramma started picking me up again."

"It's like Brad has become a robot," Andrew said. "A flesh-and-blood robot. He doesn't do anything wrong these days. He just smiles and does whatever a grownup tells him to do."

"And grownups love it," Max said.

Andrew jumped to his feet. "Come on! I'll show him to you and you can tell me if he's a Dritch kid."

They ran over to the playground. The little kids were racing around everywhere and shouting about a spider on the slide. All alone, Brad was sitting on the stump.

"That's him," Andrew said.

"Yeah," Max said. "He's a Dritch kid."

That was fast. "Are you sure?"

"He's totally a Dritch kid. They're all like that. Look over there . . . and there . . ." Max pointed out the strange sisters in the grass and a boy sitting on the bench. "There are two or three of them in every grade from sixth grade down to kindergarten. All of them are perfect kids. They never get in trouble for anything. The only time they play is when a grownup stands over them and orders them to play. But they don't quite know how anymore."

"And they never go back to how they were before?" Andrew asked. "*Ever?* Even when they stop going over to her house? I can't stand seeing him like this." Andrew never would have imagined missing Brad as he normally was, but he did.

"It doesn't wear off, not that I've seen," Max said apologetically. "There's no talking-to that goes on up there. I think it's a magic spell she casts on kids. A very powerful magic spell. Once you're a Dritch kid, you're a Dritch kid forever."

# CHAPTER TEN

**WHAT** did Mrs. Dritch do to kids when she took them upstairs? How precisely did she change them?

Andrew didn't know anything about spells or magic. Until he moved to Chills Hills, he hadn't believed such things were real. It was all make-believe for little kids.

Maybe they weren't real. Not out there. But here . . . things were different here. He had once seen a TV show about good witches and bad witches. More powerful than any witch was a sorcerer or sorceress.

Mrs. Dritch was a sorceress, and a bad one

at that. She had to be.

For days, Andrew studied her house from his bedroom window. The trees were too thick and numerous to see through in most places, but in time he learned some of the babysitter's schedule. He noted his observations on a clipboard that he hid in the bottom drawer of his desk.

She arrived at home in the spotted van by a quarter after noon.

The kids were not all the same from day to day.

Not all of the kids were Dritch kids. Sometimes there was only one.

From two to five, parents came to pick them up.

At a quarter after five, Mrs. Dritch drove away.

She returned some time later with fast food.

There didn't seem to be a Mr. Dritch, or little Dritches. She lived alone.

Until nine o'clock, she stayed downstairs and watched television.

Then the downstairs lights went off, and the upstairs lights turned on.

The upstairs lights turned off at eleven.

The light in the turret room never went on.

The list was pretty unsatisfactory. None of it was any more interesting than the things Andrew's family did. But then he thought that she had a perfect disguise. She made herself look so normal that she was boring. No one would dig any deeper.

But Andrew would.

What did she *do* to them upstairs?

One day as class ended, Andrew realized that he didn't even know if Brad had been taken upstairs. That seemed like a question to ask. Going to the front of the school, he found that his little brother was not standing with the kids at the school tree.

"Where's Brad?" Andrew asked.

He didn't know which strange sister was

which. The younger one said dreamily, "He was walking by me. Then the big boy took him away."

"What big boy?"

"I don't know. He took two or three kids away." She blinked. "It's a very nice day, isn't it?"

"Where did the big boy take them?" Andrew asked, beginning to worry.

"They went around the side of the building past Room 10."

Andrew spun around and ran past the classrooms. When he got to the end of the walkway, he heard voices. "Give those to me!" someone was saying angrily.

A kid was crying. "No! It's mine! It's my allowance!"

"You give it to me just like that dumb kid gave me his! Now, or I'll smack you!"

"Andrew?" Max called from farther down the hallway.

Andrew peeked around the corner to see

what was going on. Then he yelled so loudly that it echoed in the corridor. Wally Wonderful had three boys pressed up against the wall. The youngest one was wailing and holding coins tightly in his fist as Wally tried to pry his fingers open.

When Andrew yelled, Wally jumped and let go of the boy's hand. "Leave us alone, Bigfoot!" he snarled.

Andrew was so mad that he saw red. "You're stealing money from little kids? What is WRONG with you?"

"These are mine!" the youngest boy cried at Andrew. "My quarters for a chocolate bar! He tried to take them."

The second boy was sniffling, and the third boy was Brad. He smiled at nothing. "Did Wally take your money?" Andrew asked them. The second boy nodded with tears in his eyes, and Brad nodded while still smiling.

"It's okay," Brad said. "He needs it more than I do."

"It is not okay!" Andrew exclaimed. "Wally, give them back their money and let them go."

"Or what?" Wally said, getting right in Andrew's face. "Or you'll what?"

Wally was bigger than Andrew, but not that much bigger. Andrew had never gotten into a real fight with a predator before, but he wasn't going to back down if Wally started one. And Wally might win, but Andrew was going to make him pay for that win. He didn't care how much trouble he got into for fighting. He wasn't going to let Wally walk away with Brad's money.

"Or you'll *what?*" Wally repeated menacingly, balling his fists. Andrew did the same.

Max jumped down from the walkway. Coldly, he said, "Or I'll get Professor Beek, and the secretary and the principal from the office, and every single teacher and parent I can find. I'll have thirty people here in thirty seconds, and you can tell them why you're beating up a five-year-old for his candy money."

"Oh, you're going to tattle?" Wally said mockingly, but he looked nervous with both Andrew and Max there.

"Better a tattletale than a filthy, disgusting thief," Max said as Andrew raised his fists.

Then Wally lost his nerve. He scoffed and shoved his hand into his pocket. "Whatever. It's not enough to care about anyway." Taking out a fistful of dollar bills and change, he threw it on the ground and stalked off.

Andrew picked up the money. "How much is yours?" he asked the second boy.

"Those dollar bills. Not the coins."

Andrew gave the bills to him. "And all of the rest is yours?" he asked Brad.

Brad nodded and put the four dimes and three pennies in his backpack. As Max took the other boys out to the lawn to see if their parents had shown up, Andrew walked with Brad to the school tree. The van was stuck in traffic down the block.

This spell on him was bad. Very bad. He should have been scared and mad that someone had tried to steal his money, not happy. He hadn't even given the money to Wally because he was frightened! He had just done it because Wally had told him to hand it over.

"Brad, I need to ask you a question," Andrew said. "It's important that you tell me the answer."

"Okay," Brad said.

"The first day that you went to Mrs. Dritch's house, what happened?"

"We played."

"What did you play?"

"Board games."

Andrew was getting nowhere with this. "Did you get in trouble?"

"I got in trouble in the van for saying the music was for dumb babies. That was my first warning. And I got in trouble for playing with the hose when I was supposed to be watering the flowers. That was my second warning."

"Did you get in trouble a third time? Did you get a third warning that day?"

"Yes. It was time to study after the games and our snack. I got mad because the book was too hard. So I shoved it off the table and it hit the wall."

Andrew got down on his knees. He grasped Brad by the arms. "What happened after you got your third warning?"

"I had to go upstairs," Brad said.

Max had come over. He was listening.

"This is the most important part, Brad," Andrew said. "What happened when you were upstairs with Mrs. Dritch?"

Brad's gaze drifted away. "I don't know."

"You don't remember?"

"I went up the stairs," Brad said.

Andrew waited tensely.

"And then I came down," Brad said, and smiled.

The van stopped at the curb. Brad broke away from Andrew to go to it with the kids at the tree.

"I'm sorry, man," Max said. "There's no way to know, unless you want her to take you up there, too."

"Maybe there is a way," Andrew said, remembering his list of observations. "What are you doing later today?"

# CHAPTER ELEVEN

"**MOM?**" Andrew called. She was in the kitchen making dinner. "Shaggles keeps hanging around the front door. I think I need to take him out for a walk."

"Thank you!" Mom replied. "Don't forget to take a plastic bag. I'll save you a chili dog if you're not back in time."

It was five minutes after five, and all of the kids at Mrs. Dritch's house had gotten picked up. Putting Shaggles on a leash, Andrew went outside. They walked to the end of the block, where Max came running up. "Is . . . is she . . .

still here?" he panted. Wagging his tail, Shaggles sniffed Max's shoes.

"Still here," Andrew said. He peeked around the corner to the van parked in the driveway. "But she'll be going out for dinner soon. She always does. We just have to wait."

"Hey, big dude," Max said to Shaggles, scratching him on the head. Shaggles was so excited to make a new friend that his fanny wriggled.

At a quarter after five, Mrs. Dritch came out of her house and climbed into her van. She backed out of the driveway and drove away.

Andrew and Max crossed the street and walked rapidly down the sidewalk with Shaggles trotting ahead of them. Once they were on her lawn, Andrew tied the dog's leash around the trunk of a tree. He hid the dog behind it and said, "Lay down."

Shaggles got down in the grass. It was getting tall. Between the grass, the bushes, and the trunk, he was hidden pretty well.

"Stay."

Shaggles wagged his tail, but otherwise did not move.

"Good dog." Andrew ran to the porch.

Max was already at the door. "It's locked."

They tried the windows to the living room, but those were locked, too. Dropping over the side of the porch, they went down the driveway. The windows were too high up for them to reach.

"We could climb the tree where I left Shaggles," Andrew said. "The windows on the second floor might not be locked."

"That will be the last resort," Max said. "I hate heights."

In the backyard, Andrew tried a window and had no luck. Max hissed from the top of the steps, "Hey! This door's not locked."

He opened it and they entered the kitchen cautiously.

"How does she do it?" Andrew whispered.

No one was home, but he was too nervous to speak any louder than that. "A spell?"

Max answered back in a whisper, too. "I bet she makes them drink some kind of potion. It hypnotizes them, and then she orders them to be good all the time. Those cupboards are probably full of ingredients for it. Frog guts, spider legs, unicorn horns, human toes-"

"Gross!" Andrew said.

They opened up the cupboards. There was nothing scary inside. Salt and pepper, flour and sugar and spices, there was a glass jar of something shaped like eyeballs in the back that turned out to just be olives. Andrew opened another cupboard and found boxes of cereal, crackers, and cookies. There were two calendars on the doors of that cupboard. One listed which kids came on which days. The other had the morning and afternoon schedule, which varied except for study time at 1:30.

Max opened the door of the refrigerator and said, "Milk. Cheese. Lettuce. There's something wrapped in foil in the back."

"My mom calls those mystery packs," Andrew said. "Since they've been in there so long that nobody remembers what's in them."

"Maybe it's a pickled head or something." Max pulled it out and carefully edged open the foil. "Meatloaf. Very, very, very, *very* old meatloaf. It's getting furry. Eww."

"She's too smart for this," Andrew said. "She hides what she does. She wouldn't put her potion ingredients out in the open for anyone to see. All of her secrets have to be upstairs."

"We weren't ever allowed to go up there when I was coming here," Max said. "There was a baby gate at the foot of the stairs to remind us to keep out."

"That has to be where her sorceress stuff is," Andrew said. He followed Max through the first floor rooms.

At the baby gate, they looked up to a carpeted staircase. Dust motes drifted around in the dim light. Stepping over the gate, they crept up to the second floor. There were several closed doors going down the hallway. "Should we split up? Or go together?" Max asked.

"We should go together," Andrew said. "We don't know what's behind those doors."

A cauldron full of bubbling green soup, a monstrous snake with two heads . . . Andrew was alarmed at what they could possibly find when he turned the knob of the first door. It creaked as he pulled it open, and he looked inside with Max.

No cauldron. No monster. It was a linen closet full of folded sheets and towels.

They opened a second door. It led to a spare bedroom. There was nothing under the bed or in the closet, and all of the drawers in the dresser and nightstand were empty. As they searched for something unusual, Andrew said, "What's a ghoul can?"

"It's a can with a ghoul in it," Max said. "Opening a ghoul can in someone's room is a nasty prank. Ghouls are really destructive. They can destroy a place in ten minutes flat. Then your parents yell at you for having a messy room when it's totally not your fault. A few years ago, Jessica Finegal and Maura Miller got into a big fight over some game at recess. Maura wanted revenge, so she used a ghoul can. She sneaked it into Jessica's bedroom, hid it behind the desk, and loosened the lid. The ghoul slipped out every night and trashed the room from top to bottom. Toys and papers all over the floor, clothes ripped off the hangers and tossed everywhere, plates of old, stinking food under the bed, it was a disaster. Every day, her mom and dad shouted at her and made her clean it up all over again. The ghoul even ripped her homework to shreds and yanked the cord out of her lamp."

"Didn't it wake her up?" Andrew asked.

"Ghouls do it without making a sound, so you sleep right through it. They go back into their cans during the day to rest, so that was how Jessica caught it once she knew what the problem was. She and Maura still don't speak to each other. A lot of people won't have anything to do with Maura even now. A ghoul can is about as low as you can go. If she'll do that, she'll do anything."

"What kind of can is it?"

"Any kind." They gave up on the spare bedroom and went to the next door. "A soda can, a can of peanuts, a can of tennis balls. Big ones, tiny ones, you name it. Ghouls aren't picky. They just like cans."

The next closed door led to the bathroom that Andrew could see from his window across the street. The door after that was to Mrs. Dritch's bedroom. Quickly, they searched through it. It was as ordinary as the rest of the house.

"Maybe we're wrong," Max said.

They couldn't be wrong! Feeling desperate, Andrew went to the last door and turned the knob.

It caught.

"Locked," Andrew said. "Why would she lock a room in her own house?"

"It could have something strange in it, like that girl at school I was telling you about," Max said.

This door was different from the others in the hallway. It was made of heavy wood planks, and it had an old fashioned keyhole. Andrew twisted the knob harder, but the lock held fast. "This must go to the turret room," he said. "It's the only room we haven't seen."

He and Max took turns wrestling with the knob, but soon they had to give up. The only way this door was going to open was with the key.

The answer was in the turret room, but they couldn't get inside.

Andrew peeked through the keyhole. He couldn't make out much. Stairs? It was too dim to tell. He got down on his stomach to look under the door, but the crack was too narrow. Then he stood and pressed his ear against the cool wood to listen.

There was a sound. But it didn't come from the other side of the door.

It came from downstairs.

"Oh, no!" Max whispered. "She's home!"

# CHAPTER TWELVE

"**WHAT** do we do?" Max whispered in terror. "Oh no, what do we *do*?"

"We have to get out of here," Andrew said, looking at all of the closed doors in the hallway.

Footsteps paced around downstairs. Mrs. Dritch was humming, and plastic bags crinkled. She had no idea that they were in her house. Sneaking over to the master bedroom, Andrew opened the door and beckoned Max in.

In a whisper, Andrew said, "We can climb out into the tree from her window."

"Uhh, Andrew . . ."

"You can do it!" Andrew closed the door, and the two boys went to the window. There was a thick branch just on the other side of the glass. Sliding the window up, Andrew's heart skipped a beat when it squeaked.

The noise downstairs stopped. Filled with dread, Andrew and Max did not even breathe as they waited for Mrs. Dritch to start up the stairs to the second floor.

A long minute dragged by.

People cheered and burst out in applause. Mrs. Dritch had turned on the television in the living room, the volume carrying faintly up the stairs and through the bedroom door.

"She didn't hear it," Max whispered in relief.

The window was open almost as far as it would go. Andrew wriggled out and climbed into the tree. Shaggles looked up and whined, his tail thumping in the grass. Grasping the trunk, Andrew said, "Come on, Max!"

Max was staring down to the ground far below. His face was white. "I can't."

"You can. You have to! It's not that far."

But Max was backing away. "You go down this way. I'll sneak downstairs."

"She'll see you!" Andrew said.

"She's in the living room. I can get over the baby gate and cut into the dining room and kitchen. Once I'm out the back door, I'll run down the driveway. Meet you in your front yard." Max tugged at the window. It didn't squeak as he pulled it down.

Andrew climbed down to the ground and untied the leash. Then he and Shaggles ran over the lawn, Andrew almost hitting a jack-o'-lantern by accident in his eagerness to get away from the house.

Halfway across the street, he thought he heard a faint shout. But his shoes were scraping on the road and Shaggles was panting, a horn was honking on a nearby street, so he couldn't be sure if that was what he'd actually heard.

They had taken too long. Andrew had watched her for days and should have known better than to search the rooms so thoroughly. All she did was drive downtown to pick up fast food, and that wasn't far away. Reaching his yard, he ran behind the tree and hunkered down.

Max did not appear.

This had been a bad idea. A horrible idea. The worst idea in the history of ideas! They never should have gone into that house.

Shaggles nudged him for attention. Andrew put his arm around the dog and crossed his fingers on both hands. He crossed his toes in his sneakers, as far as they would go. *Come on, Max, come on come on come on . . .*

Max still didn't appear.

What was Andrew supposed to do? He couldn't call the police and say that he and Max had broken into a house. If he told his parents, they would be furious. He heard himself struggling to explain. *You see, we think Mrs. Dritch is a wicked sorceress who casts spells on kids to make them behave.*

Even in his head, no one believed him.

Had the yell come from Max being discovered? Or was Max just hiding in there somewhere while Mrs. Dritch puttered around her house? The yell could have been from another road, just like the honking horn.

The curtains rippled in the turret room, although the windows were closed.

Several minutes later, the front door opened. Andrew flinched and pressed up to the tree, only peeking across the street with one eye. Cheery laughter rang out. "Goodbye!" Mrs. Dritch called.

Max came out onto the porch and turned back to wave at her. "Goodbye, Mrs. Dritch! Sorry to give you a scare!"

Oh, Max was smart. He must have made up a story about why she'd caught him in her house. Walking down the steps, he headed for the sidewalk as Mrs. Dritch closed the door.

Instead of crossing the road to Andrew's home, Max turned sharply at the sidewalk and walked along it past the houses. "Pssst!" Andrew hissed.

Max didn't hear him. Since Mrs. Dritch had gone in, Andrew came out from his hiding place. He ran across the street, Shaggles bounding happily at his side. "Max! Are you okay?"

"Hello, Andrew," Max said. "How are you?"

"I'm fine," Andrew said. "What did you say to make her let you go?"

Max didn't stop walking. Andrew pulled at the leash to make Shaggles come along. The dog was dawdling at a tree.

"Do you know what I was thinking?" Max asked. "About how hard it is to pick when someone asks what my favorite subject is at school. Science and math are fascinating. But I like English and history, too. P.E. and music are fun, and I get so excited when we have a field trip. So I have to answer *everything*. I like it all." He laughed.

*Oh, no.*

Andrew grabbed Max's arm to stop him. "Max, what did she do to you in there? Do you even remember? Why did you come over here today?"

"You've been worried about your brother. You think he's changed, and that she caused him to change. But he's okay. Just trust me."

"He *has* changed," Andrew insisted. "Mrs. Dritch-"

"You've got her all wrong. She caught me in her house and she was perfectly nice. She could have called 911 or my mom and dad, but she didn't. She just wanted to know why I was there and talked to me about how it wasn't okay to go into someone's house uninvited. It was hardly even a talking-to."

It was a warm evening, but Andrew shivered. "Did she take you upstairs?"

"I was already upstairs when she found me," Max said.

"Did you go through that locked door?"

"I don't know."

"How can you not know?"

Max smiled.

It was the same smile that Brad had, the same smile that all of the Dritch kids had. Above the smile were the same empty eyes.

Max had been replaced by Robot Max.

"Hey, Andrew!" someone shouted. It was Dad, who was standing on the sidewalk in front of their house. "Dinner is on!"

"I'll be there in a minute!" Andrew called, his voice cracking.

Shaggles was on the curb, the leash stretched out to its full length. His tail was between his legs. He didn't want Max to scratch him anymore.

"*What happened?*" Andrew asked Max.

"I was upstairs," Max said, "and then I came down. I have to go home now and help my dad make dinner. It's spaghetti and meatballs night! Then I need to hit the books."

Andrew watched helplessly as Max strode away.

"Max, please!" Andrew said. "I know you're still in there somewhere. Can't you fight this off? I really need your help!"

Max looked over his shoulder and smiled that hollow smile. "It's such a nice day, isn't it? See you later!"

He had become a Dritch kid.

Andrew was alone.

# CHAPTER THIRTEEN

**IT** was midnight when Andrew woke up with a start. He had gotten away from the house without Mrs. Dritch noticing, but had Max told her that he hadn't been alone?

Andrew couldn't fall back asleep with that thought in his head. Every time he closed his eyes, he saw Mrs. Dritch creeping through the shadows between their homes. She was going to drag him back and do to him what she had done to Brad and Max, Allen and the strange sisters, and many more.

He got up to spy out his window. All of the

lights in Mrs. Dritch's house were off. A streetlamp glowed, illuminating the road and part of her yard and his. Nobody was out there.

Unless she had already made it to his house!

There would be no sleep until Andrew knew his home was secure. He picked up his baseball bat and sneaked into the hallway.

Brad was fast asleep in his room. Even the way he slept had changed. Usually the pillow and blankets were kicked everywhere, Brad sleeping upside down with his arms spread wide like he was flying, or he was diagonally across the mattress with a foot jutting over the side. His stuffed animals were normally strewn all over the bed, under him, on top of him, beside him, and spilled on the floor.

Now he was sleeping as straight as an arrow in the bed, head on the pillow and flat on his back. His hands were clasped upon the fold of the blanket. The stuffed animals were in a neat pile in the corner.

Slipping downstairs, Andrew looked into his parents' bedroom. They were also sleeping. Then he went to the front door. It was locked. So were the windows in the living room.

The back door was also locked, except for the chain. Andrew slid it on. Mom or Dad had locked the windows around it, too. Nobody could break in without making a lot of noise. Unless Mrs. Dritch had a spell for locks, but Andrew didn't want to consider that possibility.

On his way back to the stairs, something moved in the darkness. He swallowed a scream.

It was only Shaggles, who had gotten out of his bed to see what Andrew was doing. "Go to bed," Andrew whispered, patting him, and the dog obeyed.

Everything was locked up tight, and Shaggles would bark his head off if someone still managed to sneak in. He was very friendly, but he did not look kindly on strangers in his house. Even a fat, juicy steak wouldn't make him be quiet. Mrs. Dritch couldn't also have a spell for that.

Andrew fell asleep, but what he dreamed about for the rest of the night was that locked wooden door with the old-fashioned keyhole.

The change in Max did not go unnoticed at school the next morning. It upset Andrew tremendously to see his friend acting so weird. Confused by it, Casey asked Max if he was getting sick.

When they went up to the front of the room to hand in their homework, Wally Wonderful bumped into Max on purpose. Max smiled vaguely at him and said, "That's a great shirt, Wally."

During their experiment, wadded-up balls of paper kept landing on the table. Andrew saw that Wally was flicking them at Max. They bounced off his head and shoulder without

Max paying any mind. "Stop that!" Andrew hissed at Wally.

Wally didn't stop. While they filled out their lab reports, he got up to sharpen his pencil three times. He always walked very slowly past their table to check out Max's answers. Andrew couldn't guard Max's paper in addition to his own.

But worst of all was when Casey raised her hand for a scientist's fist-bump once the three of them were done. Andrew raised his as well, but Max just stared at them like he didn't know what they were doing.

"Did you hit your head or something last night?" Casey asked.

Max laughed. "No! I'm fine." There were still several minutes to the bell, and he reviewed his work instead of talking to them.

Andrew had made a friend only to lose him. And Max never would have gotten turned into a Dritch kid if he hadn't been trying to help Andrew.

All that afternoon, Andrew worried about what to do. He wished he had super-sight that would let him see into that turret room from across the street. Or if he had wings, he could fly over there and peek in.

He was glad when it was the weekend and he didn't have to see Max for two days. But he couldn't get away from Brad, who made it his mission to clean the entire house since he had no homework.

In the afternoon, Andrew went to the kitchen for a snack. Brad was sweeping the floor. "Hello, Andrew." He opened the lid of the trashcan to drop a wrapper inside.

This was going to make Andrew crazy. "Careful! That could be a ghoul can. They sneak out at night and mess up the house."

Brad laughed. "There's no such thing as ghouls."

"There could be," Andrew said. "Ghouls, ghosts, sorceresses, glowing blobs that eat cell phones, everything is possible in Chillz Hillz.

It's the most mysterious city in the world. Hear the difference, Brad?"

"Chills Hills is a very nice place. I like living here."

The doorbell rang. "Got it!" Mom called from the living room.

A happy voice made Andrew's blood run cold. "Hello, neighbor! I'm having a baking day since I'm not babysitting anyone, and I thought you might like a plate of cookies!"

"How kind of you!" Mom said.

Andrew flew out of the kitchen. In the entryway, Mom was accepting a large plate packed with cookies. Mrs. Dritch was at the door. She smiled sweetly at Andrew. "I wasn't sure what you would like, so I made chocolate chip and sugar cookies both."

"Well, we're going to like all of them," Mom said. "Would you like to come in?"

*Mom, no!* Andrew thought.

"Oh, I can't," Mrs. Dritch said. "I've got errands to run. But I did want to ask one favor. Would I be able to borrow you this afternoon, Andrew? In an hour or two when I get back from the shopping? My grass is getting shaggy in the front yard and back. I'll pay you ten dollars to mow my lawn."

Max had told her. *Max had told her that Andrew was in her house.* That was the real reason she was asking Andrew to come over. She wanted to get him alone to change him into a Dritch kid!

"I'm sorry," Andrew said. "I can't."

"Andrew!" Mom scolded. "That's a very generous offer she's making."

Mrs. Dritch chuckled and took out her keys. "Fifteen dollars then, and I'll add on an ice cream cone for when you're done."

"No, no, no, he'll do it for ten," Mom said, giving Andrew a hard look. "Won't you?"

There were several gold and silver keys on Mrs. Dritch's key chain. Andrew's eye caught on one that was much bigger than the others. It was made of brass and looked old.

He thought fast. "It's not the money. I just twisted my ankle going down the stairs this morning. Would it be okay if I came over to do it in a few days? I'm done with school at noon and can be there by twelve-thirty."

"Of course," Mrs. Dritch said in a friendly tone, although Andrew sensed that she did not like this idea as much as hers. Her house would be full of kids at that time. "The yard can last until then. Enjoy the cookies and I'll see you soon, Andrew!"

"I'm sorry about your ankle, honey," Mom said after she closed the door. "You didn't say anything earlier. Do you want me to wrap it in a bandage?"

"I don't think it's bad enough for a bandage," Andrew said. "It isn't that swollen. It just hurts a little if I walk on it too much."

Mom opened the plastic wrap and took out a cookie. "These look delicious. Here, have one!" She gave it to Andrew and carried the plate into the kitchen.

Andrew returned to his bedroom and dropped the cookie into his trashcan. He wasn't going to eat anything from Mrs. Dritch's kitchen. Taking out the clipboard from his desk drawer, he read the schedule he had made of the babysitter's day.

How was he going to get that key? It was no use sneaking in when she was doing errands or buying her fast food dinners since she would have the key with her. And sneaking in at night . . . that would be very risky. Her bedroom was right beside the door to the turret room. Even if he found the key in the darkness, he would be unlocking the door with her only a few feet away.

He read the schedule again and again and again.

And at last he saw his opportunity.

# CHAPTER FOURTEEN

**EVERY** day while the big kids did their homework at the dining room table and the baby took a nap in the downstairs bedroom, Mrs. Dritch fell asleep upon her recliner in the living room. It was only for half an hour, and then parents began to arrive to pick up their kids.

Those thirty minutes were Andrew's chance to get the keys and sneak upstairs. But he didn't know where she kept her purse. The day he had been over there studying, he hadn't paid attention to that detail.

On the walk to school, he said lightly to

Brad, "I bet you know where everything is in Mrs. Dritch's house."

"No," Brad said, looking with enjoyment at jack-o'-lanterns on a porch. "But I know a lot."

"Where does she keep the snacks?"

"Those are in the kitchen cupboards."

"What about clean diapers for the baby?"

"Those are on a shelf underneath the changing table. There are extra in the laundry room if those run out."

"Hmmmm . . . where do you guys put your backpacks?"

Brad laughed at this wonderful new game. "We put them on hooks in the living room when we get there. Then we take them into the dining room for study time. After that, they go back to the living room until we go home!"

Andrew asked the only question that mattered. "Where does Mrs. Dritch put her purse when she brings you guys inside?"

"She keeps it in the kitchen."

"Where is it in the kitchen?"

"I've seen it on the counter, and also on the chair."

Did Brad suspect that Andrew was up to anything? Andrew pretended that it was just another question in the game. "Let's see . . . what about the towels?"

Brad laughed and laughed. "Those are in the bathroom on a high shelf. T-o-w-e-l. That word is on my spelling list!"

"That's great!" Andrew said in fake amazement. "Do you want me to quiz you?"

Brad smiled. Spelling words were just as exciting as riding rollercoasters to him these days. "Yes, please!"

By the time they got to school, Andrew was positive that Brad didn't think anything about the purse questions. The only thing Brad had on his mind was how amazing it was that 'orange' was both a color and a fruit.

This was going to stop. Today!

Andrew felt that even more strongly when he saw Max sitting at their table with a blank smile. Even the ooze sensed something different in the air. It rolled around so fast that it nearly tipped over its bowl. Having just told the class to sit so he could begin his lecture, Professor Beek caught it in the nick of time. "Good morning to you, too!" he cried to the rolling ooze.

Holding the bowl steady with one hand, he opened the shoebox and took out three cell phones. He dropped them in and the ooze feasted. It was so full afterwards that it spread out over the bottom of the bowl and didn't move an inch.

Wally was eager to bother Max again during their experiment, but Casey had switched seats with him. "We're not doing all of this work just so he can copy off us!" she said.

"It's all right," Max said blandly.

"Not by me," Casey said. "What's gotten into you lately? It's always made you furious how he steals your answers in class!"

Andrew was going to fix this. He did the experiment and glanced often at the clock.

"You know what I was thinking?" Max said companionably. "We don't get *enough* homework. I wish we had three times as much." Overhearing him, several students turned in their seats to give him dirty looks.

When class ended, Andrew held up his fist as Casey passed in their work. Max stared at the upraised fist, and finally did the same.

"You're going to remember what this means," Andrew said. "I promise."

Once he was home, he paced back and forth in his room. Study time wouldn't begin until 1:30. His brain would not focus on his homework, and he was afraid that he would lose track of time if he turned on the TV.

Shaggles watched him with a worried expression on his furry face. Andrew wished that he could take the big dog along, but it wasn't right to involve him any further in this.

Look what had happened to Max! Andrew had to handle it on his own. He couldn't put Shaggles in danger.

The clock flipped past 12:30.

Then it was one o'clock.

Someone yelled outside and Andrew rushed to the window. It was just some teenagers walking down the center of the road like cars did not exist. They were taking pictures of themselves with their cell phones. As they disappeared around the corner, a woman jogged by while pushing a stroller. After that, the street was silent.

1:10.

1:15.

1:23.

1:28.

He couldn't sneak into the house at 1:30 on the dot. She would settle the kids in the dining room with their homework, go into the downstairs bedroom to check on the baby in the crib, and get into her recliner. The day

Andrew had been there, she'd fallen asleep within two minutes.

1:30.

He went downstairs. Locking the door behind him, he braced himself and looked at the house across the street. The jack-o'-lanterns leered back at him with their toothy, too-wide smiles and mean eyes.

He ran to her driveway, where he hid behind the van. When there was no movement within the house, he crept along to the backyard and stole up the stairs. The door was unlocked.

A voice mumbled in the dining room. "Six times four is twenty . . . twenty-four . . . five times seven is . . ."

The purse was on the counter. Before he went to it, he slunk to the doorway. Feet were propped up on the footrest of the recliner. Though he could not see Mrs. Dritch's face, he heard steady breathing.

He retreated to the counter and opened her

purse. A thick red wallet . . . a package of tissues . . . a hairbrush . . . a coupon for half-off at Zinky's Pizza . . . there were no keys. His heart sank as he searched through the contents of the purse a second time. They weren't there. She had put her keys somewhere else.

They weren't anywhere on the counters or the chair. Could she have left them in a coat pocket? No. It was way too warm outside to wear a coat. Or they could be on a hook in the living room.

What if they were in her *pocket?*

Then there was nothing Andrew could do. He would never be able to sneak the keys from her pocket without waking her up. He'd just have to go home and try again tomorrow.

"Seventy . . . three times nine is . . ."

The calendar said that there were only four kids here today: Brad, the strange sisters, and Grant. It was Grant's voice that Andrew was hearing. The other three were studying in total silence.

Andrew went back to the doorway. The steady breathing continued.

There was a gleam upon one of the backpack hooks. The sun was reflecting off something hanging there.

His heart pounded wildly as he edged into the living room. Mrs. Dritch was fast asleep in the recliner, her head tipped onto her shoulder.

The gleam faded. The sun had been reflecting off a metal whistle tied around the hook.

And then he saw the keys.

Right beside the recliner was a tiny table. Upon it was a plastic cup of water, an alphabet block, and the key chain.

He took a step into the living room.

Another step.

Another step.

She let out a big breath. Cold sweat broke out on his forehead.

Her eyes did not open. Taking another two steps, he reached out for the keys.

"Ten times ten is . . . one hundred. Two times twelve is . . ."

*Be quiet, Grant*, Andrew thought. Pinching the ring, he drew the keys upwards very, very slowly so they would not jingle. He pulled them back to his chest and muffled them there with his palm.

Then he took a step back. Another step and another and another, until he passed through the doorway that led to the staircase.

Dust motes drifted about in the weak light, just like they had when he'd been here with Max. Taking a huge step over the gate, he climbed up to the second floor. Grant's voice faded away.

Trembling, Andrew went down the hallway to the tall wooden door. It was hard to make his feet go forward when what he really wanted to do was run out of this house and never come back for as long as he lived.

He selected the big brass key and slid it into the keyhole. When he turned it, there was a click.

Andrew opened the door.

There was another staircase here, but this one was shorter, wider, and without carpet. Up at the top of the steps was a very strange shimmer of light.

The house was as quiet as a grave behind him. Forgetting about the keys, he went in and pulled the door mostly shut. The shimmer disappeared, and was replaced by many dull twinkles. A bad feeling made the hair rise on the back of his neck. He wanted to go home.

Max.

Brad.

And Andrew himself. If he did not go up there now on his own, he would become like them after she dragged him up.

There was no choice. He climbed up the stairs.

# CHAPTER FIFTEEN

**ALONG** the wall of the round turret room were bookcases. They rose halfway up the windows and there were no books in them. Every shelf held snow globes.

That was it.

That was all there was in this room, dozens upon dozens of snow globes on splintered wooden shelves. Snow globes and doily curtains and a bare floor. Sunlight pierced through the curtains and twinkled on the dusty glass of the orbs. In a corner was a closet. The door was ajar, and within a box inside were more globes.

There were no potions or robots or monsters up here. There was no sorcery, because there wasn't such a thing as sorcery outside of movies, cartoons, and books.

Mrs. Dritch was just a babysitter after all. Andrew had been wrong about her. Whatever had caused Max and Brad to change . . . the answer had nothing to do with this room. She just had her knick-knack collection up here, and a locked door to keep the kids out so they wouldn't break anything.

He stood there in disbelief.

It was too dangerous to sneak back through the house and return the keys to the table. Not dangerous because of some magic. Dangerous because of how long he would be grounded if she caught him and turned him over to his parents. Andrew was going to get out the way he had the first time, through her bedroom window to the tree. He would leave her keys on her nightstand and hope she thought she had put them there herself but forgotten.

*Snow globes.*

He stepped to the closest bookcase to look at them, expecting to see tiny Christmas trees and snowmen upon mounds of fake snow. The dust was so thick that he could not see into any of them. He picked one up. It wasn't attached to the black pedestal that it was resting upon. Rubbing off the dust with his thumb, he spied a figure inside.

It was a girl in a red dress. Her head turned to Andrew as if she were alive. Then she ran over to pound on the inside of the glass with her small fists. Her mouth was open like she was shouting, but Andrew didn't hear anything.

She *was* alive.

He set down the snow globe and picked up another from its pedestal. Rubbing off the dust, he looked in to a boy in a tiger costume. Shocked to see Andrew, the boy ran to the glass to pound on it just like the girl had.

Again, Andrew could not hear him. But the boy's lips were forming the word *help*.

Andrew set down the globe and looked around the room frantically. There had to be two hundred orbs in the bookcases altogether! Or more!

One of them had to hold Brad, but there wasn't the time to search through every single shelf. Swiftly, Andrew rubbed off two orbs. Neither held his brother.

Something moved on the ceiling as he reached for another globe. A gust of wind was circling around the light fixture. As it lowered, it made the curtains flutter.

Andrew backed away in fear. This was no normal wind.

It spun in circles, and then it flew down the stairs and passed through the small crack in the door. Relieved that it was gone, Andrew returned to the bookcases.

The dust on these orbs had to have built up over many years. Andrew searched the shelves for cleaner snow globes. There was one on a bottom shelf. The glass was almost completely clear. Dropping to his knees, he picked it up.

Brad wasn't inside.

Max was.

"Max!" Andrew exclaimed. The tiny figure of Max stared up to Andrew in astonishment and began to shout.

This was Max, the real Max! No empty smile or vacant eyes, he fled to the glass and pounded on it. *Andrew, Andrew*, he mouthed. Andrew held up the globe, seeking a way to open it and let him out.

Someone was humming.

Footsteps came down the hallway. Mrs. Dritch had woken up and was now upstairs!

And the keys were in the door to the turret room.

Maybe she wouldn't see them there, or that the door was cracked open. She might have just come upstairs to get something from her bedroom.

The humming and footsteps got louder. Tucking Max's orb under his arm, Andrew looked in panic to the windows. He could not get out from here! The bookcases were pushed up against each window, and they were heavy. Even if he could shift them, they would scrape on the floor. Also, there weren't any trees out there.

The only hiding place was the tiny closet. Andrew stepped into it. No clothes hung from the bar. There was only that box of globes, which left just enough room for him to stand beside. Closing the door and hunching beneath the bar, he looked through the slats.

Keys rattled.

Mrs. Dritch hadn't gone to her bedroom. She was now coming up the stairs.

Andrew held his breath as Mrs. Dritch appeared in the turret room.

"Hello, my lovelies," she said in a sweet

voice, tucking her keys into her pocket. "Did someone come up here to bother you?"

She would think Grant had done it. He was the only one of the four in the dining room who could have.

That strange wind had returned to the room. It swirled about Mrs. Dritch and floated up to the ceiling. She paid no attention to it whatsoever. Going to a bookcase beside the closet, she bent to look behind the globes. Andrew did not even blink.

"Any left over here, hmmm? No," Mrs. Dritch said. She went to another bookcase farther away and pushed the globes around. "Any pedestals back here, darlings? I thought I still had some."

Then Max's orb squirted out from under Andrew's arm.

He tried to catch it. The tip of his finger even brushed the glass. But he missed, and it hit the floor where it shattered.

Mrs. Dritch bent over double like she had a

sudden stomachache. "Oh, dear!" she said.

The small figure of Max was not among the pieces of broken glass at Andrew's feet. A white light lifted from the floor. It shot upwards, past Andrew's legs, past his chest, past his face, and flew straight through the ceiling of the closet.

Mrs. Dritch straightened. She was going to find him now.

But she didn't come to the closet. She pushed up onto her tiptoes and reached for a top shelf. "There we are!" In her hand was an empty pedestal. She brushed it off on her shirt.

The wind went around and around on the ceiling.

"All right, Andrew!" Mrs. Dritch called in good humor. "Pick up one of those empty orbs and bring it out here."

# CHAPTER SIXTEEN

**ANDREW** picked up an orb and opened the closet door. His knees were shaking.

He needed a plan. He just didn't have any time to come up with one.

"Come, come, come!" Mrs. Dritch said. Although she was smiling, her voice was a little impatient. "Your mother will be here soon, so we don't have much time!"

"You're an evil sorceress," Andrew said.

Mrs. Dritch raised her eyebrows at his accusation. "Oh, no. Oh, no, no, no, dear boy. Does this look like the home of a sorceress to you? Where are my toadstools and frog eyes?

Did you happen to find a magic wand anywhere?"

"You're still evil, whatever you are!"

"How am I evil?"

"You change people into what they're not. You take away-"

"I take away unhappiness, Andrew. That's it. Unhappiness causes naughtiness, and naughtiness causes more unhappiness. All I do is give the gift of happiness to children, and happiness to everyone around them."

The wind was gusting faster around the ceiling. "You took away my brother and put some . . . some robot-like kid in his place!" Andrew cried. "I want him back the way he was!"

"You want him to be in trouble at home, to get poor grades in school? To always be mad at the world?"

"Yes! Well, no, but yes! That's who he is!"

"Forgive me, but those don't sound like the wishes of a loving older brother. You should want the best for him." She pointed down to the floor. "And who he is now, downstairs and hard at work at my table, is his very best self."

Mrs. Dritch gestured to the snow globes. "Here all of that unhappiness is trapped! And think of how wonderful it will be when you, Andrew Calistoga, can walk out that door with your unhappiness forever behind you as well."

When he tried to go around her, she blocked the stairs.

"Let me out of here!" Andrew demanded.

Her voice became hypnotic, and her eyes pierced into his. "How good this will be for you, how easy it will make your life. You will never be rude or thoughtless or angry with anyone. You will never be grounded again, because you won't ever do anything wrong. You will never get distracted when you're studying, or be tempted to cheat on a test. In the morning when you look in the mirror, you will like what you see. You will spend every minute of your day working hard, but it won't feel like work at all!"

Andrew gripped the empty orb tightly. He was going to throw it in her face and run for those stairs! Pulling back his arm, he attempted to throw the globe.

It stuck to his hand like it had been glued there. "What's going on?"

"You're really very lucky," Mrs. Dritch said as he shook his hand. The globe did not drop. "A few more years and it would have been too late for you! There's nothing I can do for unhappy grownups, but children . . . I am their spirit of *joy*."

The wind was no longer gusting around the ceiling. It had dropped down to Andrew, where it encircled him and whipped about very fast. The curtains shook in the windows.

"When this is all done, you will thank me," Mrs. Dritch said in conviction. She was standing outside of the wind and watching in pleasure.

Andrew would thank her because he would no longer be Andrew. He pried at the globe. It would not come free. Not only that, but now his other hand was stuck to the glass, too!

"No!" he shouted, feeling a pull in his chest to the snow globe he held. He was going to be drawn inside and put on a shelf, there to sit forever and ever. Dust would collect on the glass and blot out the world while his robot self washed the dishes with an empty smile.

He took a step back. The wind followed him, going even faster.

Mrs. Dritch laughed. For all of its tinkling sweetness, it was an ugly sound.

Andrew stepped back again and hit a shelf. His elbow jostled a snow globe.

The pulling sensation grew stronger. He was going to be trapped, but Max wasn't trapped anymore. Andrew could smash a few more of these globes before he went into his orb, and hopefully one would belong to Brad.

He jerked his elbow, knocking snow globes off the shelf. He kicked at those on the bottom. Glass shattered and white lights shot up to the ceiling. The laughter came to an abrupt halt.

"Stop!" Mrs. Dritch said, doubling over in pain.

It hurt her when they broke! Andrew screamed in anger and attacked the shelves with all his might. She lunged for him and he darted around her. Sweeping his elbow along a middle shelf, he knocked six orbs to the floor. They made loud smashes and sent up their freed lights. Most went through the ceiling. One dove through the window.

The pulling sensation vanished, and the wind wasn't going so fast around him now. Andrew kicked and elbowed globes as fast as he could. The one stuck to his hands let go all of a sudden.

As Mrs. Dritch lunged for him again,

Andrew leaped away. He caught hold of the tallest bookcase and pulled hard. Globes rained down to the floor and broke, followed by the whole case. It was so old that it came apart. White lights went everywhere like a swarm of lightning bugs.

The wind around Andrew vanished. Mrs. Dritch flickered. She *flickered*, like someone had turned off the switch that powered her and turned it back on a moment later.

She wasn't smiling or laughing anymore. She was in a rage. "You must stop!"

Andrew dodged her to pull down the bookcases. Two of the orbs didn't break, so he picked them up and threw them at her. One bounced off her leg and broke on the floor. The second flew straight through her, since she had flickered. It hit the closet door and smashed to bits.

The turret room was a mess. The floor was covered in broken glass and pieces of wood. Andrew spotted another unbroken orb and stomped on it. The light shot through his foot and up to the ceiling, where it disappeared. Out the window, it soared away over the street.

"You will not get rid of me this way!" Mrs. Dritch shouted.

She was there, she was not there, she was there yet he could see through her. When she lashed out for his shoulder, her fingers passed through his body and came out the other side.

There was one bookcase still standing. Andrew brought it down.

"Nooooo!" Mrs. Dritch screamed.

It hit the ground with a deafening crash, and she vanished for good as the lights flew up to freedom.

*Brad*, Andrew thought. He ran down the stairs and through the house.

There was giggling from the dining room. Andrew burst through the doorway. "Brad!"

The strange sisters were strange no more. They had stuck pencils up their nostrils. "See?

I'm a vampire!" one said. Grant shushed them, but he was laughing.

Brad was still studying.

Andrew felt like someone had kicked him in the gut. It hadn't worked.

Unless he'd missed an orb. Taking the stairs two at a time, he fled back to the turret room and overturned the remnants of the bookcases. There was only broken glass beneath them. He ran to the closet and dumped out the box. But all of those globes were empty.

Then he saw an unbroken snow globe under a window. Andrew scooped it up and looked inside.

*Brad.*

Brad was in a little ball, his arms wrapped around his knees. He was crying. When Andrew tapped on the glass, his brother did not look up.

"It's going to be okay," Andrew said. *Please let it be okay.*

He dropped the orb.

The glass broke.

A small white light rose from the pieces. It flew to the stairs, Andrew running after it down to the hallway. He followed it to the first floor and to the dining room, where it lifted to the table and raced across it.

Brad turned a page in his spelling workbook and bent over it studiously. The other kids were gone, all of them shouting in the backyard as they played.

The light went into Brad's chest. It blew him back into the seat. Stunned, he sat there and blinked in confusion.

Andrew bent down by the chair. "Brad?"

Brad stared at him. "*Andrew?*" He looked at the pencil in his fingers, and the workbook on the table.

Then he made a face. His nose crinkled up and his eyebrows lowered as he glared at his homework. "I hate spelling."

Andrew laughed. His brother was back.

# EPILOGUE

**IT** was the day of the big science test. First there would be the written part, and then they would do the experiment. The team that earned the highest score would get to take the ooze home for the rest of the summer. Professor Beek was worried that it might get lonely all by itself.

If they won, Casey would take the ooze to her house first. She could only have it for a few days since her family was going on a long vacation. Then she would give the ooze to Max, who could have it for a week. His young cousins were coming to visit at the end of the week, and he was afraid that they would let the ooze out. Andrew would have it after that until the first day of school. He couldn't wait to show it to his family.

They wanted to win the ooze. They had studied very hard. All of them were determined to keep Wally Wonderful from cheating off their tests and winning the ooze for himself. As they took their seats, Max pulled out a little can of cat food from his backpack. A lot of tape pinned down the lid. He grinned and passed it to Andrew, who placed it at the end of the table.

It only took a minute for Wally to notice the can. "What's that, Bigfoot?" he asked suspiciously. "Hey, Big-stupid-foot, what's that?"

"A ghoul can," Andrew said. "So you don't look at our papers."

Wally snorted. "There's no ghoul in there!"

The can trembled.

"No *way*."

The can slid across the table's edge and

shook violently.

Wally couldn't see that Max had a hand in his backpack. There was a remote control toy in the can.

"Maybe you're thinking that you could just look around the can to our tests," Andrew said. "And yes, that wouldn't be hard. But, if you do that, I'm going to make it my personal mission to get this ghoul can into your bedroom. Your *second* bedroom."

The blood drained out of Wally's cheeks until he looked like a ghost. "You don't know where I live!"

"I do," Casey said brightly. "314 Acorn Drive."

"So do I," Max said. "Go up the stairs and the second bedroom is three doors down on the left."

Wally grew even paler.

"This can is pretty small," Andrew said, tapping on the lid. The can shivered. "And I'm really good at hiding things. It will take you a long time to find it in there. Too bad for your stuff."

The can slid to the end of the table and fell off. Andrew caught it as Wally backed away fast. "Get that away from me!" Wally said in horror.

Andrew replaced the can on the table. "Good luck on your test! I hope you studied."

It was plain from Wally's face that he hadn't. As Professor Beek handed out copies of the test, Wally went from white to gray.

Max made the can shake one more time as a final warning. "This was such a good idea," he whispered to Andrew. The three of them fist-bumped.

The way to scare a predator was with a bigger predator. A ghoul was so small that it could fit into a tiny can, but it had a lot of power. A lot more power than Wally Wonderful had.

After school ended, Andrew and Max shouted goodbye to Casey as she carried the bowl with the ooze to the curb. The ooze seemed happy to be outside of the classroom. It was sliding around everywhere and glowing extra bright.

"It will be like having a pet for a week," Max said in excitement. "I can't have any. My mom is allergic to everything."

"I found a busted cell phone in the street the other day that I'm going to feed it when it's my turn," Andrew said. "It's in my desk at home."

Brad had already gotten picked up. His new babysitter was a normal woman who had two big jungle gyms, a sandbox, and a giant trampoline in her backyard. Andrew had gone over there with Brad and their parents to check it out. All of the kids were regular kids, and the one who was in trouble for kicking sand got a real talking-to.

When Brad came home from there, he was always himself. Sometimes that was good. Sometimes that was bad. Andrew still couldn't think of much to do with his brother. He got frustrated so easily and stormed away, because he was trying to be perfect like Andrew. But Andrew wasn't perfect, no matter what his little brother thought.

Max craned his neck to look for his grandmother's car. "Oh, she's stuck down there at the end."

"I'll wait until she gets here," Andrew said.

"It was bugging me last night," Max said. "What Mrs. Dritch said to you when she was disappearing. It won't get rid of her."

That bothered Andrew, too. "But her house is still empty. I'd know if she was back. A real estate agent came yesterday and put a FOR SALE sign on the lawn."

"Then maybe she was lying. But what *was* she?"

"What do you mean?"

"Witches, sorcerers, they're still human," Max said. "They have bodies. But she told you that she wasn't doing sorcery, and she didn't leave a body behind. Was she a ghost?"

"She called herself a spirit."

"A bad spirit." Max grinned as Wally Wonderful slunk to his car. "I saw his test when Professor Beek was handing them back. He failed. Big time."

"We got him good."

"Yeah. I'm going to bring that ghoul can to school every week as a reminder, if he and I end up in the same class again. I'm not running a charity with my grades. They're *mine*."

Andrew hoped that Mrs. Dritch had been lying. "Chills Hills is a strange place. Chillz Hillz, I should say."

"Wow, is it ever," Max said, and went to his car.

Later that afternoon, Andrew had an idea. He searched through the garage for the batting tee and was pulling it out just as Mom drove up with Brad.

"I don't like using that!" Brad said

grouchily the instant he got out of the car.

"It's not for you," Andrew said. Shaggles tagged along as Andrew carried the tee to the front yard.

He set it down beside a bucket of balls. Putting one on the tee, he readied the bat on his shoulder.

"You don't need the tee," Brad said jealously. "You can hit without it."

"Even the best players do drills with a tee," Andrew said. "They work on their stance and their swing and it helps them get better. I need to do these more often."

Brad watched as he practiced. He missed a few times on purpose. Once the yard was littered with balls, he carried the bucket around to pick them up. When he came back to the batting tee, he set it down and said casually, "I have to rest my arm for a minute. Do you want a turn?"

"I need to drill, too," Brad said.

Andrew stood to the side as Brad swung.

The ball flew across the street and rolled into the gutter. "I smacked it so far!" Brad yelled.

"You did. I'll get it," Andrew said.

As he crossed the road, a strong breeze blew past. It moved aside the branches of the shaggy trees in front of Mrs. Dritch's house.

The smiling though unfriendly jack-o'-lanterns were gone. Now there were four pumpkins that hadn't been carved sitting around the tree trunks. Someone had stolen the carved ones.

But why would a person steal them yet put regular pumpkins in their place? Or had the real estate agent just swapped them? Jack-o'-lanterns didn't last forever. They could have been going bad.

Maybe it was nothing.

Maybe it was something.

It was Chillz Hillz, after all.

"Did you see that?" Brad yelled. "Andrew, did you see that? I hit it all the way into the next yard!"

"Good job!" Andrew said.

Brad beamed. "It's your turn for a drill. I have to rest my arm, too!"

They were just pumpkins. Nothing more. Everything was fine.

Andrew turned away to play ball.

COMING SOON

## Chillz Hillz #2: Don't Be Late

# ABOUT THE AUTHOR

Kerrigan Valentine lives in California with her partner. She divides her time between writing, occasional teaching, seasonal viticulture positions and learning how to cook with limited success.